the Last Table in the Sun

LEXIE CARDUCCI

Cover image by:
Book design by: SWATT Books Ltd

Printed in the United Kingdom
First Printing, 2020

ISBN: 978-1-8382288-0-4 (Paperback)
ISBN: 978-1-8382288-1-1 (eBook)

LexieCarducci
Torquay, Devon
TQ2 6TL

Prologue

Olivia aimed the remote at the telly and changed the channel from MTV's Greatest Hits to Sky News and there it was, the confirmation they had been dreading. The red banner flashed at the bottom -

'Partygoer who fell from rooftop of Mayfair Hotel is pronounced dead at the scene.'

Chapter 1

'There's nothing quite like a fresh start.'

L ondon. The City of... Well. Just about everything, really! Whether you're an aspiring entertainer, training to become a doctor at Imperial College, a hairdresser with the passion to be the next Jamie Stevens or an expat from down under taking advantage of your two year visa before you hit the big three-oh. Waiters and banker wankers alike all sharing the same skyline, everyone is welcome in London and everyone can make new starts.

Bay smiled as she contemplated that thought, a new start. She exhaled, physically releasing the tension that had been carried on her shoulders the last two months. Her breakup with Henry at the beginning of the summer had crushed her. She'd been with her university sweetheart for nearly ten years and when he'd taken her to their favourite spot in the Cotswolds for a weekend getaway, she'd been sure it was to propose, but it was in fact the exact opposite. It was her own version of the

Warner / Elle Woods split in *Legally Blonde* and she'd been completely blindsided.

Despite having the unusual name Bay, Bay herself was not that unusual. In fact, she considered herself downright ordinary, if not, dare she say, boring! Until now, everything had casually fallen into place with no drama and no wrong turns. She went to university like most other 18-year-olds after they completed their A Levels (other than the ones that took a gap year, or let's face it, extended holiday courtesy of the bank of Mum and Dad). She had the university boyfriend who she'd fallen in love with at Exeter University's freshers' week on an animal themed fancy dress night at Cavern Club. She'd been a slutty mouse like Karen in *Mean Girls* and Henry was a parrot, wearing a costume meant for a 12 year old that left his chest exposed and was far too tight around his crotch, which really brought the term 'budgie smuggler' to life. As cliché as it sounds, it really had been love at first sight and they'd been inseparable for the next nearly-decade.

After her three years studying journalism, Bay had started work at the local newspaper back in Watergate Bay in Cornwall where she grew up. She and Henry moved in with her parents and Henry got a job in project management at a large housing development being built on the outskirts of the town. Not much had changed in the next few years. When Henry had broken things off, they'd both still been living with Bay's parents and both had stuck with the same role at work: no promotions, no saving for a deposit, no real progression in life at all. She'd always imagined she'd marry Henry, at the Watergate Bay hotel of course, they'd have three children (a boy and two girls - James, Henrietta and Lacey - yes they had actually planned these finite details) and they'd live happily ever after in their 1950s terraced family home, which of course would need completely renovating. They'd get as far as putting in a new Ikea kitchen and then blowing the budget on mod cons that were upsold at the checkout, such as a wine cooler that would change colour, a tap that boils water because kettles were redundant these days, heated floor tiles and to top it off a Miele coffee machine good enough for Starbucks. The rest of the house would look like utter shit but hey - you'd have a limited edition Smeg fridge! She'd seen it happen to her friends; it was the norm and she had been completely ready to indulge suburban life.

Yet there she was, stuck in traffic on the M3 in her Fiat 500 (cappuccino coloured, obviously), full to the brim with her life packed up into Safe Store boxes, on her way to one of the world's busiest cities, to restart her life, at 28 years old. It had been her friend Olivia's idea for her to move to London. Olivia had been there for ten years now and Bay had visited her Fulham flat a handful of times. The girls had known each other from nursery school where Olivia had cut the hair of one of Bay's Barbie dolls into a sharp bob, a sign of her future fashion ambition as Olivia had followed her styling career to Southampton Solent - only to find herself, as many do, floating around in the world of PR in London.

A job in which no one really knows what you do. Even Olivia herself always seemed rather vague about her role. Olivia was *always* pretty vague about everything, unless it was a celebrity sex scandal, in which she somehow seemed to have more information than even the tabloids.

In Watergate Bay, Olivia had been rather bland just like Bay, with her thin shoulder length hair that was somewhere between blonde and brown but not in that fashionable blondette way, in more of a midlife crisis mum way. She'd had pale skin, a wonky, toothy smile and was verging on the overweight side of the BMI scale. However, within a year of her moving to the big City and pushing every PR connection she could blag, she now resembled something out of TOWIE, with her tanned toned bod, sleek black extension clad hair and pearly whites, in fact pearly *straight* whites that would make any American envious.

Bay pulled up outside Olivia's flat on Mimosa street, which was apt as Olivia was pretty much a fully-fledged alcoholic. As if on cue, Olivia sprung out of the front door waving a bottle of Moet around like it was a trophy. 'Welcome to London, baby!' she screamed, far too loudly for 11am on a Tuesday. Bay couldn't resist a smile. This was a good start and as bonkers as Olivia was, she felt grateful to have such a good friend. A friend that would take a day off mid-week to help you settle in. Although not a friend that helped with your luggage, apparently. Bay dragged her electric-pink suitcase (that wouldn't look out of place on a flight to Ibiza) up the stairs, its wheels clonking loudly on every step and the handle becoming looser with every pull.

'Hurry up, Cinderella!' Olivia called from the open flat door on the second floor. Despite her lack of assistance with the suitcase, Olivia had redeemed herself by already pouring the Moet into two rather fancy gold champagne flutes and instantly thrust one into Bay's hands as she crossed the threshold into flat three.

Olivia's flat was just like Olivia; neat and tidy like a show home but with a wacky splash of colourful artwork on the walls, perfectly injecting her sense of fun into the atmosphere. It smelled like she had just walked into The White Company. A pink velvet couch took centre stage in the living room with a leopard print cushion, a tall cactus tree sat in a gold pot in the corner, a pink fluorescent neon sign hung on the wall of the open plan kitchen that read 'cocktails' and then there it was - the piece de resistance - the limited edition Mickey Mouse Smeg fridge.

Olivia clocked that Bay had seen her extravagant piece. 'Only 90 of those made,' she threw the comment away as Olivia did when she intended to impress, nonchalant yet aimed to induce envy. Bay had to grin though with the familiarity of the sight of such a fridge, maybe London wouldn't be too different from home after all.

'So how was the drive, babe?' Olivia cut into Bay's thoughts and just as she was about to answer, Olivia chimed up again. 'I don't know why you insisted on bringing your car, *no one* drives in London!'

Bay wrinkled her forehead in silent disagreement as she glanced out of the window at the overcrowded street below. She'd driven around the block twice before a mum in a Chelsea Tractor had zipped out of a space without even checking her mirror, and Bay had just as quickly darted in.

'And don't even get me started on the parking wardens.' Olivia was on a rant once again. 'They'll *literally* hide in bushes while you park up and dash into Waitrose to grab some oat milk, you'll barely be gone for a minute and *bam!* They'll have slapped a ticket on your windscreen. It's almost worth paying the £2.20 for half an hour of parking to ensure these crooks don't make a penny off you.' She snorted in disgust.

'£2.20 for half an hour, bloody hell, really?!' Bay nearly spat out her Moet over the pink velvet couch. If she wasn't heading for broke before, she was certainly going to be getting there a hell of a lot faster now. Olivia shot her a look as if she thought Bay might actually have let a champagne droplet touch her precious sofa and she scanned said sofa for evidence before responding.

'Bay, seriously, you didn't put money on?'

'No,' Bay replied, with a puzzled look.

Olivia rolled her brown eyes as she sprung up and peered out of the window 'What did I just tell you? They are like vultures round here. I once got a ticket in the time it took me to walk to the friggin' pay machine.'

'But at home I don't think I've ever even seen one, they're like mythical creatures designed to threaten us into paying for parking, which we don't of course because they are never around!'

'Well I learnt this the hard way when I first got to London, they certainly aren't mythical here, take a look, there's a lesser spotted dick wad hovering around your car.' Olivia pointed as she grabbed Bay's face and shoved it against the window glass which had a perfect view as it was, of course, spotless. And there outside, stood by her cappuccino Fiat, was a uniformed parking warden, complete with hat, tapping speedily into the electronic machine strapped around his neck.

Both girls hurtled out of the door, Bay picking up pace as Olivia told her the price of a parking fine was £65 which was to double if not paid in the given time. Bay couldn't afford to start off her new London life in minus numbers. £65? That's a good night out right there!

'Oi, we're just leaving!' screeched Olivia in her best authoritative bitch voice. Bay wasn't sure this was the right approach to start a conversation with the person who controlled the fate of your next £65 but - hey ho, Olivia had already set the tone.

'Sorry, ladies, but you haven't paid, and I've already processed the ticket, can't undo it now,' smirked the warden. At least he'd had the courtesy to start with 'sorry' supposed Bay.

'Bullshit!' yelled Olivia, scrambling at the bit of paper being printed from the warden's machine.

He had a sinister grin on his face like a Disney villain who had just hatched an evil plan and Bay was fast regretting ever considering being nice to this jobsworth.

'Get in the car,' Olivia demanded, moving to her next tactic and she started tugging at the passenger door. 'It only counts if he puts it on the windscreen and takes a picture,' she added, as they both got in the car. In her haste to get in, Olivia had thrown Bay's neatly packed boxes into the back and clothes had toppled out everywhere.

The warden had heard her, which wasn't surprising as Olivia's voice was the loudest and shrillest you'd ever hear, and it became a race against time as the warden shoved the printed paper into a high vis packet. Meanwhile, Bay had gone back and forth about five times to squeeze out of the space, her vision impaired by the boxes Olivia had half shoved into the back. Olivia was now sat amongst the other half of her clothes, most of it being Bay's underwear - typical that it had been that box! Just as Bay lurched forward for the final time to clear the car in front, the warden slapped the ticket on the windscreen.

'Not today, Satan!' barked Olivia, hitting the windscreen wipers, which threw the parking ticket onto the street. The ticket man lowered his camera in disappointment as Bay glanced in the small gap she could see out of the rear-view mirror. She turned her eyes back forward again, where Olivia gave him the finger whilst lassoing a pink thong that had fallen out of the underwear box in the air in victory and gave a 'whoop'. An elegant older lady gave them a look of half disgust and half support from the sidewalk.

'Thanks, Liv. I would have just stood around and accepted the ticket like a moron,' Bay said, turning onto Fulham Road.

'I know, that's why I'm here to guide you, moron!' replied Olivia, almost kindly. 'It's only a matter of time before London brings out your inner bitch. I can't wait to meet her!' Olivia's all-too-familiar cheekiness appeared in her eyes.

'So, shall I just go back round the block and park up?' asked Bay getting a little nervous in the London traffic without a sat nav to guide her.

'No, no, turn right here.' Olivia waved her hand and Bay had to dart into the correct lane.

'What about your flat, did you lock the door? You don't have your bag,' quizzed Bay, ever the sensible one.

'The door self-locks and I leave a key in the plant pot, too many lost on a night out! And I love a Birkin bag as much as the next girl but everything we need is on our phones nowadays, you really are living in the dark ages back home! Anyway, we're already late, we're going to Chelsea. I've got a surprise for you!'

Chapter 2

'Life is too short to have boring hair!'

Although Chelsea was only the next town along from Fulham, in the London traffic it took them nearly 30 minutes. Olivia breathed a continuous stream of impatient huffs and puffs on the drive like a dragon stuck in a queue, although Bay knew she secretly enjoyed being chauffeured around so she wouldn't have to sit on the crowded 22 bus with people who, to quote Olivia, 'hadn't been on a decent shopping spree since 1999'. Bay was pretty sure Rihanna took the tube to her own gig once though, and she's the queen of demanding attention. And Olivia wondered why she herself was so often described as high maintenance.

Chelsea was like the boujier, taller, skinnier yet fuller breasted big sister of Fulham and its inhabitants were just as glamorous and pristine. The girls with their long, flowing locks and perky assets tottered along the King's Road in their red-bottomed heels while the gents were less suited and booted but still hunky in their tweed blazers, ironed chinos and moccasins, looking like they had just walked out of an Abercrombie and Fitch interview (and obviously nailed it!). The stores of the King's Road were a mix of quaint boutiques and up-market chain stores like Zadig and Voltaire and Sandro but unlike the tourist gift shops of Watergate Bay they were flooded with people. Bay felt a rush of excitement sweep over her as the unmistakable buzz of city life filled her with energy.

'So, where are we going, Liv?' she asked for the fourth time to an unresponsive Olivia who was tapping away on her iPhone. 'Liv?' she tried again, this time a little louder.

'Hmm?' Olivia mumbled as she arose from her zombified state of mobile phone hypnotism, and she blinked a couple of times to acclimatise her eyes back to daylight. 'Oh, shit! Sorry, we've just driven passed it. Turn left here. Sorry, hun, I was miles away. I mean, I tell the office I'm taking the morning to meet a client, yet they still find the time to email me some shit to deal with. Bike,' Olivia nonchalantly added, as Bay was about to turn left.

'Jeez!' Bay flinched as she automatically slammed on her brakes. 'A little more urgency next time please, Liv. Where did he come from, anyway?'

'Twats, the lot of them,' Olivia cussed as she mimicked a cyclist. 'They think they own these streets, yet do they stop at red lights or acknowledge people's indicators or stay in their dedicated supercycle highway lanes that cost us London taxpayers a fortune to build? Nope!'

Bay pulled into a parking space whilst Olivia continued her rant. After the close encounter with the parking warden earlier in the morning, Bay didn't fancy taking her chances again and returned to the car with a paper print out ticket from the machine just as Olivia finished muttering something about reflective jackets and light up helmets with fairy lights on. Bay nodded as if she'd been listening and then followed Olivia back up to the King's Road.

'So, can you tell me where we're going now?' asked Bay, just as Olivia's phone started ringing.

Olivia put her finger up to silence Bay as she answered the call. 'Alex, yeah we're literally outside,' she snapped as she grabbed Bay's hand and whisked her across a zebra crossing and into a Tiffany-blue fronted hairdressers called *Duck and Dry*.

'Have you ever been on time, Olivia?' questioned a bald-headed man with a thin moustache as the girls entered the shop. 'Do you even know how it feels to be early, darling? You should try it sometime,' he teased, as he air-kissed Olivia.

'As a matter of fact, Alex, yes I was two minutes early at a spa once and it was the most boring two minutes of my life!' Olivia had such a charming way of shutting someone down. 'This is Bay, she's staying with me until she figures out her life, she's new to London.'

'Yes I can see that,' Alex replied, looking Bay up and down before lifting up a strand of her rather limp hair and then dropping it like he'd just removed an offending fly from a drink before discarding it to the floor. 'So, she's willing to do anything?' he asked, completely ignoring the fact that Bay was stood right in front of him and was quite capable of responding for herself.

'Well, she's not that kind of girl!' snorted Olivia and her and Alex guy threw back their heads with laughter like a pair of drunk hyenas. 'But yes, I have brought Bay here today as she's in need of a fresh London make over, she's all yours for the next few hours. Surprise!' she yelled, turning to Bay and throwing her hands up in the air. 'Alex is one of my clients and he's just started working with this new hair extension brand and before I approve them for our books, I of course need to see the finished result. So, Alex, what colour are you thinking?'

'Let me grab the book, babe, I'll be two shakes of a dog's tail,' said Alex. He jerked his bottom from side to side, which Bay guessed was supposedly meant to resemble a dog shaking its tail. He then skipped off down a set of stairs, clapping his hands together like a 4-year-old who'd just received a new dress for her Barbie doll.

'Liv, I, well, I'm obviously really grateful but...' Bay chose her next words carefully. Disagreeing with Olivia Buttersby was never a smart move; Bay had learned that in primary school when she disagreed that Baby Spice was the best Spice Girl. Olivia had banned Bay from sitting with her in the cool seats at the back of the school bus for a week! 'I just don't want to lose my hair, I like the length it's got to.'

'Lose your hair? Sweetie, you're getting a full head of bonded human hair extensions which would cost you nearly a grand! All the celebs have them and if they're good enough for Cara DeLevingne then they're bloody well good enough for you!' Olivia opened her eyes wide, raised her eyebrows and tilted her head sharply towards Bay as if telling a child that they were not allowed to watch another episode of *Peppa Pig*.

Bay was pretty sure that C DeLevingne had a bob now but the thought of having a celebrity-worthy mane of hair was far more interesting than correcting Olivia on her Cara DeLevingne blunder.

'Champagne, ladies.' Alex wafted through the room like a fine eau de parfum as he returned carrying two champagne flutes.

Bay had never been to a hairdresser where they served alcohol. It was something she had assumed was staged for the cameras on *Made In Chelsea* and yet here she was on the same turf as the affluent poshos on the telly. On their very stomping ground, in fact! Despite the fact that she was already on her second glass of bubbles of the day and it wasn't even 1pm on a Tuesday and she had to drive home later, she couldn't bear saying no.

They toasted and just as they were about to open Alex's book of colours, the doorbell jingled and in walked two girls; one blonde and one brunette, both taller than the entire line up of the Victoria's Secret summer fashion show standing on top of one another. As the brunette removed her Chanel sunglasses, Bay immediately recognised her. It was her first celebrity sighting in London - well, if you could count washed up *Love Island* stars from four years ago as celebrities.

Bay had heard from friends that in London you could walk past a celebrity every day and not even recognise them. All they needed was a sports cap, sunglasses and casual attire; it was a fool-proof disguise as far as they were concerned.

Just as Bay was about to grab Olivia's arm in excitement, the brunette started waving in their direction and then proceeded to run over and hug Olivia. Once all the cooing and the cheek kissing had finished, Olivia made the introductions.

'Bay, this is Mia and Molly.' She quickly turned her attention back to the two girls. 'What are you guys doing here?'

'We're here for a blow,' replied Mia, the tanned, brunette, sort-of-famous one.

'Aren't we all!' quipped Alex, thrusting his hips towards the giggling girls like he was in some sort of *Magic Mike* line up, before disappearing again to get what Bay could only presume would be more champagne.

'Bay, that's an unusual name. Like Bey as in Beyonce, or as in "I'm gonna Netflix and chill with Bae"?' asked Mia, smiling with her perfectly aligned teeth.

Bay was supposedly named after Watergate Bay, or so she was led to believe. She hoped this was in fact the truth and that it was not actually after the Bay of Islands where her parents had honeymooned and as a result, she appeared nine months later. She really didn't want to divulge this in her first conversation with Olivia's friends, talk about TMI! Luckily one of the girls jumped in.

'As in Bay - meaning auburn hair, right?' suggested the blonde, Molly.

'Really, how do you know that's what it means?' Mia asked suspiciously as if her friend had just plucked the idea from thin air.

'Because my mum's friend is called Bay because of her auburn hair.' Molly flicked her blonde locks behind her in victory. She may as well have added a 'Duh' onto the end of her sentence.

'Interesting...' Olivia hummed to herself as she flipped through the pages of the hair colour book and reached the shades of red.

'Ginger!' Bay grimaced, as she screwed up her face in horror.

'Ginger is not a colour, sweetheart, it's a food!' Alex's voice boomed through the salon and Bay resisted replying 'Tell that to Geri Halliwell'.

'What a fabulous idea, though! It'll really make those green eyes *pop!*' Alex clapped his hands together with approval, making everyone jump.

Bay spent the next hour having her entire head painted with dye that resembled the colour of a tomato. She was afraid she may end up looking like Rihanna circa 2010 but fortunately by the time it was washed and dried, the colour had settled down to a softer tone ala Amy Adams. Alex had then taken 1cm thick strands of long, silky, auburn coloured hair from a reel of hair extensions, brushed the ends over what looked like a glue gun and stuck it to the roots of her own hair before using a rubber bit of rectangle-shaped material to roll the hair together into a tiny bond. It was all very artistic but probably the longest procedure ever known to mankind! Although over the course of five hours it did give her the opportunity to get to know Olivia's friends better.

Blonde Molly was a 26-year-old socialite from old money London that swanned around the streets of Chelsea for a living, as she'd never have to work a day in her life thanks to her great-grandfather's invention of frozen food back in the 1920s. Who knew that discovering freezing your meats could provide a lifetime of income for the next few generations? Bay wondered how Molly's great-grandfather, rest his soul, would feel about Iceland.

Molly lived just off the King's Road in an eight-bedroom house which Olivia had described as being worth about £20 million. Bay knew London was a property bubble on its own, but when you could buy a brand new five bedroom detached house on ten acres of land for well under a million in Cornwall, 20 million for a pokey townhouse the Victorians had assembled which hadn't seen a new plumbing system since pulling a chain was a thing, seemed a little steep. Molly loved to travel and although it was only June, she'd already been on seven trips abroad, one of which was to Bali where she had met current boyfriend Archie.

Brunette Mia on the other hand, Bay had a little bit of an idea of her story, as like most 18-30 year old's she had been sucked in by evening telly and devoured the 2014 series of *Love Island*. Mia was originally from

Italy which explained her olive skin and thick, dark hair. Since being on *Love Island* she'd had a steady stream of income from brand endorsement deals, TV appearances and adverts. However, being the ancient age of 30 and 2014's news, she was struggling to keep afloat in the sinkable waters of fame. Hence why she had employed Molly's boyfriend Archie as her new manager to try her hand at acting, much to the bitter disappointment of Olivia who quite fancied moving into the celebrity agent game.

'And... Voila!' sang Alex as he spun Bay round in her chair and whipped out a mini mirror to show her the back of her hair whilst spritzing a bottle of hairspray like there was no tomorrow. There literally *would* be no tomorrow with the sheer amount of pollution he had blasted into the atmosphere.

Bay was startled when she saw the fully finished version of herself in the mirror. Her hair was a beautiful shade of deep rust with flickers of chestnut. It glistened like the sun's reflection bouncing off the sea and sat in naturally wavy curls either side of her face and down to her stomach. She knew that looks weren't everything, but she had certainly not felt this self-assured and confident in a very long time.

'Right girls, let's head to the Sloaney for a celebratory drink!' chimed Mia. Brilliant, more unnecessary drinking. 'Come on, come on, I have something exciting that I've been dying to tell you about!'

Following Mia's cue, the four girls, after their obligatory exchanging of triple cheek kisses with Alex and an

Instagram photo, tumbled out of the salon and headed to the pub, eager to hear the big secret Mia was about to share.

Chapter 3

'The best friendships are built on a solid foundation of alcohol, sarcasm, inappropriateness and shenanigans.'

Olivia had suggested that Mia and Molly Uber to the famous watering hole, the White Horse in Parsons Green, also known as 'The Sloaney Pony' to locals.

Since there would be no parking in the vicinity, Bay and Olivia had taken the car back to the flat. Now that the parking restrictions for residents had finished at 5pm, they were safe to abandon the Fiat, still packed to the brim with Bay's boxes.

'So, how do you know Mia and Molly?' Bay asked, as they walked through the residential Fulham streets.

'Well, Mia used to be a client at the PR firm until she went vegan and as a result McDonald's decided to stop giving her endorsement deals of free burgers every time she dined there. And Molly has been a friend since my clubbing days in the City. Obviously, I introduced them!' Olivia always talked about her clubbing days as if they were 30-odd years ago and she was an ancient dino-saur incapable of busting a move on a dancefloor - yet in reality it was only three years ago when she used to party five days a week and not the twice weekly event it was now, albeit accompanied with a round of Xanax. Olivia clung to her days of being 25 like a five-year-old clinging to its mother on the first day of school. To be fair, the Botox was doing its job and she'd probably get away with still looking 25 for the next few years at least.

As if Olivia could hear Bay's thoughts, she ducked down by the side of a parked car and began assessing her face in the wing mirror, pulling at her forehead as if it wasn't tight enough and crease-free already. It was, in fact, about 1mil away from looking like Joan Rivers. She slathered her lips in a clear Mac gloss and smacked them together before giving her reflection a cheeky wink.

They finally turned the corner to the Sloaney Pony, which was now spilling onto the streets with 20-some-things chattering away, pints and Proseccos in hand. Although it was only early evening, the place was abso-lutely rammed with people: those lucky enough to finish work before 6.30pm, freelancers who worked from anywhere they weren't kicked out of for ordering an espresso every four hours, and those that, like Molly, probably didn't need to work at all.

The day had transformed into a bright evening and the sun had yet to set. They pushed through the crowd until they spotted the stunning blonde and brunette holding the fort on a round table still bathed in sunlight in the seating area at the front of the pub.

'Nice one, girls, the last table in the sun as always!' grinned Olivia, swinging a leg over the wooden bench whilst simultaneously helping herself to a glass of the Prosecco that was cooling in an ice bucket.

'That's right, age before beauty!' joked Molly, waving her empty glass at Olivia to signal a top up.

'Pfft, you can help yourself with that sly remark!' Olivia returned the joke, pretending to place the bottle back into the holder before laughing and topping up the other glasses.

Bay took her glass and sipped it gingerly. Although the bubbles were refreshing on the summer's evening, she hadn't consumed so much alcohol throughout the day since Christmas 2012 when she was asked to help out with her aunt's addiction to Archers by assisting with the drinking of it. Little did Bay know that it was a liquor and was supposed to be mixed with something else. Needless to say, the majority of the bottle was regurgitated at various points throughout the roast luncheon. Bay tried to shake the horrific memory, but she could already feel the effects; skipping lunch in the day hadn't helped either and she was now starving. The BBQ behind them was producing the most wonderful juicy-smelling smoke that wafted towards their table, carried by the light summer breeze.

'Mmm, I could murder a burger,' drooled Molly, also catching a whiff.

'Eurgh! And a murderer you would be!' Mia bit back in disgust.

'Oh, Mia, please, like your Jimmy Choos aren't 100% cow leather. And you call yourself vegan!' Molly rolled her eyes as she took another swig of Prosecco.

'Yeah, Lindsay Lohan will be pictured eating a chicken wing next week and you'll be down to KFC quicker than you can say "nuggets" to be part of the next trend,' chimed in Olivia with a cackle.

Bay didn't know whether to laugh or change the subject quickly to prevent World War Three. She didn't understand how so called BFFs could slate each other so much and still be sat round the same table pouring each other's drinks, but as Mia joined in laughing with the other two girls Bay decided that bitchy banter must be the new friendly and all four of them giggled and clinked glasses.

'So, what's this big secret then, Mia? You're banging a One Directioner?' Olivia raised her eyebrows as much as the Botox would allow.

'No, even better!' Mia said, excitedly.

'I don't know, that one with the big hair was pretty good!' Molly said with a wink.

'Glad the word that followed big there was hair, Mol!' Mia returned the wink at her friend.

Olivia nearly choked on her Prosecco, 'No? Stop it!' She was barely able to control herself when new gossip came to light.

'Hey this is *my* story!' Mia interrupted, steering the conversation back to her.

'OK, go on then.' Olivia turned her attention back to Mia.

'So. You know I've been trying to get into acting now...'

'If you call seductively drinking a can of coke and posting it on Instagram acting, sure!' Olivia teased.

'And thanks to my Archie!' Molly raised her glass to her boyfriend's apparent success.

Bay began to see that the girls interrupting each other constantly was a common theme to every conversation. She wondered if they would ever find out what this secret was.

'Well, it's taken him six months to get me an offer that's nothing to do with being a bikini extra but yes, I guess, thanks to him. But seriously, yesterday I auditioned for the female lead in, wait for it...' Mia did a little drum roll on the table. 'None other than Carl Baker's new film *The Trouble With Us*.' Mia opened her mouth and eyes in a shocked expression waiting for her friends to join her in their response.

'Carl who?' Molly gave a puzzled look.

'Sweetie, if it's not Karl Lagerfeld I'm not interested!' Olivia made shooing waves with her non-Prosecco-wielding hand.

'Oh my God! That's amazing!' piped up Bay, with excitement of actually being able to get involved in the conversation.

'And *you* know this Carl guy, how?' questioned Olivia.

'He's the director of *Christmas Bells* and *One More Dance*, he's originally from Cornwall!' Bay said, knowledgeably.

'Yes! Thanks Bay, at least one of you has a brain,' smiled Mia.

'Ooooh, tell us more! Wait! Wait! Top up first!' squealed Olivia as she hastily replenished the glasses. 'Drink up!' she instructed, seeing Bay's glass with the same level of Prosecco as ten minutes ago.

'It's a romantic comedy about a couple who keep breaking up,' said Mia.

'So, it's a story of your life then!' Olivia and Molly chuckled to each other like schoolgirls.

It was a well-known fact, well if you read the *Daily Mail*, that Mia was always 'on the rocks' or 'pictured having an argument' with her current boyfriend Max. Mia chose to ignore her still-giggling friends and acknowledged Bay's focus instead. 'It's filming later this year across the UK *and* it's a six-figure fee,' she dropped in at the end.

Olivia and Molly stopped laughing, 'No way, shut up!' barked Olivia, whose ears always pricked up at the mention of money - particularly a large sum of it.

'And you'll never guess who's up for the lead role?' Mia continued, pushing her silky brown hair behind her ears, proudly, 'Bachelor Ben!'

All the girls suddenly became interested in Mia's possible new venture with Bachelor Ben, the nickname for one of the UK's hottest, wealthiest actors, known more for his stunningly good looks and ability to carry off a topless beach scene than his actual acting skills.

'Was he at the audition?' Olivia was practically swooning. 'Did you have to kiss him? *Touch* him?' Olivia had clearly been putting her own little fantasy together in her head as she yelled rather too loudly even in the busy pub. An uneasy-looking blond male quickly edged away from their table.

Mia silently took another sip of her Prosecco.

'You minx!' cried Olivia, spotting the shy look in Mia's eyes that meant she had definitely done something she shouldn't.

'Isn't he slightly less of a bachelor now?' Molly reminded everyone, to alert them to the fact that he was now engaged.

'Talking of eligible bachelors...' Olivia raised her glass to two men walking towards them.

One Bay recognised as Max Merrygold, son of billionaire property developer Michael Merrygold. Their faces were always popping up at parties and fundraisers in the back of *Hello!* Magazine. Max, like his father, was a walking Ken doll - but not in the creepy-looking human Ken doll man, more of the traditional actual plastic Ken doll where you always enjoyed taking his clothes off when dressing him in a new outfit more than you probably should have as a kid. Yes, Max was like the Ken doll, tall, toned and tanned with dark hair. He was wearing navy jeans and a red check shirt over a white T-shirt and tan Chelsea boots, clearly a stamp on his postcode.

That left the other man as Molly's boyfriend and Mia's agent, Archie. Archie creepily looked more like Molly's brother than her boyfriend; they had the same big blue eyes and pale yet perfect complexion and heaps of blonde hair sprouting from their heads. Bay self-consciously pulled her new auburn locks in front of her as a reminder that, she too, now had envy-inducing hair. It was working and she gave a smile back to Archie whose gaze had lingered for a good few seconds.

'Another round?' Archie asked, with a wink.

'Need you ask?' Olivia pursed her lips and with that the men disappeared towards the bar.

'So, who's up for *Mahiki* tonight then?' asked Molly, grinning mischievously.

'Ooooh!' Olivia clapped her hands together.

'Hmmm...' Mia was a lot less enthusiastic about the idea.

Bay wondered why everyone was getting so excited by something that sounded like a Japanese sushi dish, and what was so exciting about take-out in the week. She thought that was what people did in London as the tiny kitchens really weren't equipped to cook full-blown meals. The other girls obviously realised Bay wasn't on their page by her cloudy, blank expression.

'It's a bar, Bay,' explained Mia.

'Well, more of a club!' Molly took the evening from a midnight finish to a 2am finish.

'On a school night?' Bay immediately regretted asking the question. She wasn't doing herself any favours trying to shake her reputation as 'boring Bay' like the popular girls had nicknamed her in school. Plus, the fact that she didn't even have a job yet meant it really didn't matter what day of the week she decided to get shitfaced.

'School nights are the best, babe! Only the riff raff go out on the weekends, we can actually get to the bar in under 20 minutes and the bar staff have the time to make a proper martini and not one that's three quarters ice. *And* no one has to pay the extortionate table fees!' Molly smiled as if she had been giving evidence in court, making a very valid and convincing argument.

'Not that you're ever the ones paying though, right?' Archie landed a kiss on his girlfriend's head as he and Max returned with another bottle of bubbles.

'That's the whole point of being a girl! We get into clubs for free, we get the tables for free and guess what - we get the drinks for free, too!' Olivia popped the cork off the fresh bottle with her thumb, so it shot off across the road, narrowly missing someone's Porsche that was parked outside.

Bay slowly sipped her topped-up glass, the bubbles popping up and jumping at her face, wetting it like that light drizzly rain that doesn't warrant an umbrella, yet still ends up getting you drenched. The drinks made her relax a little and she shut her eyes as the last bits of sun started to dip behind the trees to the west, and she listened intently to the cackles and chitter-chatter of her new world.

'Oi!' She was rudely interrupted by Olivia jabbing her in the ribs with her extremely bony elbow and waving Bay's still half full glass in the direction of her face. 'Drink up, the cars will be here soon.'

Bay obeyed her friend and guzzled the remnants of her chalice, just as two blacked-out Mercedes pulled up. Ah, UberX, thought Bay, having watched every celebrity get out of one at *The Television Awards* on telly last year, and now here she was, in London about to get in one herself. She could barely contain her excitement about such a trivial thing as getting into a car.

'Ladies,' said Max, ever the gentleman, opening one of the doors for the girls. 'Archie and I will take the other one, we know how you girls love a good gossip on the way to the club.' He laughed and shut the door once they were in.

'Hey, Mr Taxi Man, we need to make a quick pit stop on the way,' instructed Olivia as they pulled away.

'We do?' questioned Mia, looking a little fed up about her arrival time to the club being delayed.

'Of course! Unless you think *Mahiki* is going to let you in the VIP area looking like that!' Olivia looked her friend up and down. 'I've got a whole rack of stuff from one of our brands that I need to take to a photo shoot tomorrow, sat in my hallway. I mean, just sat there begging to be worn! Better yet, taken to a dance floor in Kensington. As long as you don't spill red wine down them, I'll allow you all to borrow a piece. For tonight only, ladies!'

The girls jumped out of the car at Olivia's. 'We'll be five mins,' said Molly to the driver as she looked at her watch.

To everyone's surprise, particularly the taxi driver, they were actually only a few minutes. These girls were pros at getting in and out of an outfit in 20 seconds flat. Quicker than a catwalk model at London Fashion Week, thought Bay, as she clambered into a sequined number. They had also perfected the flick of liquid eyeliner and the zhushing of hair that gave it that sexy 'I woke up like this' look. They all arrived back to the car, minus Olivia.

'Oh, for fuck's sake! There's always one!' Molly rolled her eyes in the direction of the door to Olivia's building.

'And it's always Olivia!' Bay felt a small pang of guilt as she dissed her current best friend but a bigger pang of warmth as her other two new friends laughed along.

Olivia appeared a minute later at the window of the cab and, after seeing Mia had now joined the girls on the back seat, realised she would be left alone to sit in the front. Typical Olivia always managed to turn everything around to make out like she gets what she wants. 'Guess I call shotgun then!' She hopped upfront next to the driver. 'Sup drives?' She winked at him and then cranked the volume up on the radio. 'Let's get this party started!' she hollered, and then passed a bottle of already-opened champagne to the girls in the back. 'One for the road!'

'No drinking!' The driver waved his hands, angrily.

Olivia pulled a £5 note out of her purse and placed it on the dashboard. 'Do we look like the kind of girls that want to waste champagne?'

The driver snatched it up.

'Didn't think so!' Olivia grinned as Mia took a swig from the bottle and handed it to Bay.

Bay poured it into her mouth and as the cold liquid trickled through her body she wondered if, not even a day into London life, she was becoming an alcoholic. However, she was in too deep tonight already and as she passed the bottle back to Olivia, she couldn't help but wonder what the rest of the night had in store.

Chapter 4

*'If you want to know an answer,
ask them. If you want to know
a secret, get them drunk.'*

They pulled up outside the Kensington Garden Hotel. Bay recognised the prestigious area right next to the club as Kensington Gardens, leading to Hyde Park. They were basically partying next door to Wills and Kate! The Uber driver made no effort to open the doors for the girls and to Olivia's obvious annoyance she had to clamber out on her own accord. As Olivia fumbled for the door handle and outstretched a freshly tanned leg towards the pavement, there were big flashes of lights.

'Oh good, Rupert is here on time,' she said, reaching for her clutch bag, and missing her footing, nearly flashing the entire band of waiting paparazzi. The flashes got quicker as she did so, followed by a wave of disappointment as they realised it wasn't Mia who was about to reveal what she had for breakfast!

'Oh, for God's sake, Olivia, I thought we were having a quiet one, not one that will end up on the *Daily Mail* sidebar of shame!' Mia growled, realising her PR friend had given the paps a heads up on their evening out.

'Well, I've got to advertise these outfits one way or another,' responded Olivia, composing herself for the cameras.

Mia took a deep breath before exiting the taxi. Olivia helped her out, grabbing Mia's hand and gently pushing her forward into the ongoing strobe lights of cameras, like an equestrian presenting their show pony. Olivia then linked arms with Mia and they strutted straight passed the queue, who were now also snapping pictures and turning their heads to see what all the fuss was about, and glided to the entrance of the club like a couple of swans.

Bay felt slightly nervous, although she still managed to give a flicker of a smile to the cameras as Molly grabbed her hand and they were ushered into the club by a security guard. This was a completely new world for her and she kind of loved it, so far.

Inside the club it was already buzzing. The smell of sweet alcohol mixed with Tom Ford perfume was pushed around the room by the scantily-clad, skinny girls in their 20s dancing the twostep along to base-heavy rap beats. It was so hot in the club that Bay could just about excuse the lack of clothing people were wearing. Groups of young men (some who looked like they would be IDed for cigarettes in Tesco) hung around low, white, glossy table booths nodding in the direction of the girls. It was like a pick'n'mix for them to choose which girls would pass the audition stage to be invited to join the men at their table.

And, just like that, one of the crisp-white-shirted men got up from his caveman stance and headed over to two blondes doing their thing on the dancefloor. One was bent over doing what could only possibly be described as twerking, whilst the other one was filming her, probably for an Instagram story. The man tapped the girl filming on her shoulder and her friend got up from humping the floor to join the conversation. The man then slipped his hand into the small of each girl's back, claiming his prizes like the sleazeball he probably was, and escorted them back to his table. The other girls, already guzzling Grey Goose vodka mixers at the table, were clearly annoyed at the new recruits as they each glanced them up and down from their blonde, curled hair to their stiletto shoes before turning their backs on the new girls and grabbing the humongous bottle of vodka from its cooler on the table and proceeding to put it into each other's mouths. The other men at the table suddenly perked up and began cheering. The new girls started twerking again as the competition for attention and alcoholic rewards hotted up and would probably be how their night continued.

Bay's observations were interrupted by a change in music as 50 Cent's *In Da Club* began playing and she was nearly pushed to the floor by a parade of girls in black leather swimsuits and masks who strutted by carrying bottles of glow in the dark Dom Perignon with sparkling candles wedged in the top of them, followed by a group of topless men with abs popping out of their stomachs, manoeuvring what could only be described as a giant treasure chest with the same sparklers, four bottles of Grey Goose, numerous shots, a whole coconut and about 20 paper straws which would soon disintegrate with the sheer amount of alcoholic liquid present on the masterpiece. The display itself, which rivalled Macy's Thanksgiving Day Parade, was delivered to a table at the back where the men flexed their steroid-gained muscles and the girls (or table whores, as Olivia described them), reached for the alcohol like they had just been let into a shoe sale at Harrods.

'There they are!' Olivia pointed, nearly whacking one of the topless waiters in the face as she strutted towards a distant Archie and Max at a table in a cordoned off area at the back of the club. It looked like the boys weren't alone - they ushered two girls up off the table when they saw their girlfriends approaching. Mia gave Molly an eye roll and Molly grabbed her friend's hand for support.

'What's going on?' Bay asked Olivia, as the two girls passed them on the steps, almost brushing shoulders.

Olivia shook her head and rolled her eyes too at the same time making her look like some kind of deranged cat, particularly with her flicky eyeliner. It was weird for Olivia to not be vocal about a situation.

Meanwhile, Mia had shaken off Molly's hand and had made a bee line for Max. Bay could tell from Mia's body language that she was upset, but she couldn't hear them. Eventually Mia picked up a half full glass left by one of the two girls and threw it in Max's face before storming off back into the melee of the dance floor.

'That's why you don't piss off Italians!' Olivia cackled, as she sat at the table, reached for the vodka and four glasses and began pouring. She caught Bay's eye and patted the seat next to her. Bay sat down on command. Molly sat in the other corner in a private discussion with Archie and Max had disappeared, presumably to search for Mia or to dry off his dripping face, one of the two!

'More music, less drama!' Olivia raised her glass to toast Bay. They clinked glasses and simultaneously took a sip from the candy-cane-coloured paper straws.

Bay nearly spat hers right back out, 'Bloody hell, Olivia, want some orange with that vodka?' she asked, stifling a laugh.

Olivia gave one of her cheeky winks before removing her straw, knocking back her entire drink and pouring another, equally as strong. Olivia had finished three in the 30 minutes they had sat there by the time Bay had even drunk two thirds of hers.

'Bitches!' slurred Olivia, slapping Bay's thigh in a slapstick cowboy way... but it still kind of hurt.

'Who?' quizzed Bay.

'Amy and Ruby, that's who!' Olivia gestured towards the dancefloor, spilling dashes of vodka and orange juice over Bay's legs as she did so. Bay made sure to dodge the drips to avoid any stains on the expensive, borrowed garment she currently wore.

'What, those girls that were here?' Bay asked, remembering Olivia would blab about anything after a couple of drinks.

'Amy Braybury is jealous of Mia! Even tried to do her hair like her, and wear Mia's style of clothes. Her dad might have bought her part in Corrie and Downton but she'll never get the acting parts like Mia does. Too boring! No matter how much she tries to hit on Archie, there's no way he'd represent someone with *no talent!*' Olivia waffled between sips of her drink.

Molly came over and joined the girls from her conversation with Archie, took Olivia's drink right from her hands as she was distracted by taking selfies on her phone and began drinking it herself. Olivia looked around dumbly to see what was happening and to see why she no longer had a drink in her hand.

'Everything OK?' Bay said gently to Molly.

'Yeah, they were just talking property stuff with Max. Amy's dad, Richard, and Max's dad both work in the industry,' explained Molly, coolly.

Bay expected that it was something a little more than 'property stuff' and clearly so did Olivia as she had shot Molly one of her 'you're not fooling me' looks.

Molly sighed, knowing she had been rumbled by Olivia. 'He has been acting weirdly recently, like he's on edge about something.'

'What could it be about?' asked Bay, wanting to comfort Molly. Olivia was always useless in these delicate situations.

'I don't know, I've tried bringing it up to see if he's OK but he just snaps at me.' Molly took another sip of her drink.

True to her insensitive self, Olivia then proceeded to rant about her various bad experiences with men.

Bay excused herself from the table to take a trip to the ladies before Olivia had the opportunity to start bleating like a goat again. Bay almost wished Olivia would just pass out like one of those silly fainting goats, too. She never did know when to stop! On her way through the club, she began piecing the bits of information together. So, one of the girls that had been chatting to Max and Archie was Amy, a brunette who was, as Olivia described, very similar in appearance to Mia. The other girl, Ruby was a model, almost the spitting image of Naomi Campbell, with legs up to her armpits! Amy's dad, Richard, was also a successful property developer like Max and his father Michael.

Bay nodded to herself, feeling pleased with her ability to piece it all together even after a couple of alcoholic beverages. As another topless waiter walked out of a private room, holding the door open for his other topless colleague carrying a tray of empty glasses, she spotted Mia sat at a table inside with none other than Bachelor Ben. Stopping, she took a step back so her back rested against a wall. Well, they are about to work together, she thought as she joined the queue for the ladies. Then she spotted Archie and Amy, the brunette, having a heated discussion by the club entrance and heading her way.

'Leave her alone. And me for that matter. I'm not the only agent out there, Amy, go and find someone else to sign you because it sure as hell won't be me! You're in direct competition with my client and you've tried on multiple occasions to undermine her. You may think you're a threat to her, Amy, but you're just a cheap knock off and soon enough you'll be yesterday's news. Without the talent that Mia has, you really won't be around for much longer.' Archie was calm in his delivery, yet brutal in his words.

Nevertheless, Amy seemed not to care and argued back. 'I'm younger and hotter, Archie! You just watch this space, I'm gonna be the next big thing!' And with that she gave two fingers to Archie, flicked her long hair and headed back towards Ruby who was bopping from side to side on the dance floor.

'God, I need a cigarette,' huffed Archie to himself as he headed off towards the smoking area.

The door to the private room opened again next to Bay, and Mia poked her head out to look around. She came face to face with Bay, jumped in shock and then beckoned her into the room. Bay headed inside, although a little reluctant to leave the queue she'd spent the last ten minutes finding and the last two minutes standing in.

As if reading her mind, Mia said, 'Don't waste your time there, you could be there for days, it's pretty much empty in here.' Mia put her arm around Bay as they walked into the private room and showed Bay to the bathroom.

When she returned, Mia was sat down at the table she had been at with Bachelor Ben, although he was nowhere to be seen. The private area was like one of those fancy, exclusive members clubs. The music was still thumping and there were only about half a dozen people sat at various lounging areas which had a black and gold theme.

'So, what was that about?' asked Mia. When she saw Bay's blank expression, she dug a little deeper. 'Archie and Amy, I could hear them from here when I opened the door earlier, but I didn't want them to see me.'

Bay paused for a moment to assess the situation. Was she about to gossip or spread a rumour about two people she barely knew anything about based on a conversation she could just about hear? And, as Mia had said, if she could hear them from the entrance of the private room why was she now asking Bay to divulge her version of events? Bay decided she had no loyalty to Archie or Amy for that matter, but she did value her new friendship with Mia, so morals aside she decided to spill the beans.

'I heard Amy trying to get Archie to be her manager too, but he said you and her were too similar and there'd be no point representing competitors in the industry. Oh, and then he said how talented you were and that basically she had none and wouldn't be around for much longer.'

Mia smiled a little bit with her lips tight and leaned back in her seat. 'No talent is a little harsh, but she has got it easy. Her dad pretty much paid off her drama school to get her in and his company rebuilt the new Corrie set so I'm sure that had something to do with her coincidentally appearing on it.' Mia shrugged.

'And her dad works with Max's dad, is that right?' asked Bay

'*Wrong!*' barked Mia. 'Complete opposite, they work *against* each other, they are both property developers and are often competing for sites, it's such a cutthroat industry!'

'You of all people would understand a dog eat dog world. Was that Bachelor Ben you were with?' Bay asked, the alcohol in her body making her much more forward than she usually was, and her journalist skills took over. She physically took a step back, realising she may be prying too much into Mia's life. After all, they had been having a private conversation in a private room.

'Oh yeah, just about our second audition tomorrow. Oooh tell you what, what are your plans tomorrow?' asked Mia, brightly, making Bay feel less like she had been prying and more like she had been a concerned friend.

'I'll be somewhere between unpacking my life and trying to find a job,' Bay laughed.

'So, nothing really then, why don't you come with me to the audition? I hate going on my own, then we can go for afternoon tea afterwards. Oh, please, Bay. It would really calm my nerves!'

Bay looked the leggy brunette up and down. Her perfect pearly white teeth grinned at Bay, and her big brown eyes glistened in the club lights. Bay wondered how someone so faultless in appearance could be so anxious about anything. If Bay possessed even half of Mia's attractiveness she'd strut through life without a worry. Of course, if Instagram has taught anyone anything, it's that life really isn't all it's made out to be in the highlights reel; the glossy exterior can often be a mask for an entirely different interior. But still, when the UK's next up and coming starlet invites you to accompany her on an audition for a role that could solidify her name in showbiz, issues or no issues, secrets or no secrets, you simply say yes and go! And that is exactly what Bay agreed to do.

Or so she thought.

Chapter 5

'Criticism is not nearly as effective as sabotage.'

They left the club about half past midnight and the group went their separate ways. Molly and Archie left first, followed shortly by Mia and Max whose explosive tempers had calmed down after a few more shots of whatever strawberry liqueur it was they seemed to be offered on tap. Bay and Olivia were in another Uber on their way home and Olivia had surprisingly begun to sober up.

Olivia was perfectly proportioned although she was big boned, but in her new physique, thanks to crash diets, online weight loss pills and a lot of Pilates, she never looked fat anymore. But it did mean she could hold a lot more drink than Bay. If Bay had consumed as much as Olivia she'd need carrying out of the club. Thankfully, Bay knew her own limits and both were feeling rather spritely for nearly 1am on a Wednesday.

They arrived back at the Fulham flat and both looked at the boxes still in Bay's Fiat, waiting to be unpacked.

The girls looked at each other and at the same time both said 'tomorrow'. They laughed and climbed the steps to the flat.

'So, Mia invited me to her audition tomorrow,' Bay said, waiting for Olivia's opinion on the matter.

'Great, you can come to work with me first thing. Mia's coming to the office at 11 before the audition to drop her and Molly's dresses back, so you can meet her there.'

'Perfect!' responded Bay, deciding her friend was probably too tired to give any form of opinion on Mia's audition or the Amy situation.

Without further ado, they both said their good-nights and headed to bed.

Bay awoke the next morning to the sun trying to squeeze through a gap in the curtains. Olivia insisted on having blackout curtains and a slither of sun had sneaked in through the gaps at the sides. Bay was used to leaving her curtains open at home so the natural light would wake her early and she'd be greeted by a view of the sea each morning. She drew the curtains to a different scene this morning, one of pretty Victorian architecture, white-fronted grand buildings with black and white tiled steps leading to pastel coloured front doors and covered with sprawling purple wisterias. The light hum of the traffic even reminded her of the crashing of the waves. It was pretty in a different way from the seaside and Bay decided to embrace the change in scenery.

She glanced at the wall clock and gasped, it was 8.30am, probably the latest she had got up on a weekday, like... ever. She rushed into the living room to find Olivia sitting cross legged on the fluffy grey rug in a pool of sunlight with her laptop on her lap.

'Oh, I thought we were going to your work early?' Bay asked, looking at Olivia, who was as laid back as ever.

'Welcome to my office!' replied Olivia without even looking up. 'They are pretty relaxed. I can work where I want as long as I actually get the work done.'

'Wow, and they trust *you* to work from home?' Bay prodded fun at her friend as she took a seat on the sofa.

'They think I'm collecting some more clothes for the shoot this afternoon, but you know, trust is trust and I'm bloody good at what I do!' Olivia smirked. 'Now pop the kettle on, we'll take some coffee to go. Oh, and grab your dress from last night.'

Bay did so and returned to the living room with the sequined number she had worn the previous night. Olivia proceeded to spritz the garment with a fruity smelling spray and puffed a few bits of hot air from her plug-in steamer over it.

'Good as new,' she said proudly, holding the dress up to the light. The sequins glittered in the sun, reflecting a disco ball pattern across the room.

The girls got ready, filled up a couple of refillable eco-friendly thermos flasks with coffee (because Olivia said in London if you weren't seen to be eco-friendly someone would probably punch you in the face) and then jumped on the 22 bus towards Sloane Square via the King's Road. It was surprisingly quiet on the bus, although it was way past rush hour now. Bay thought this must be Olivia's tactic for handling public transport, by leisurely commuting to work at a reasonable hour after everyone else had slummed it in cramped conditions.

Olivia's office was just behind Sloane Square station, a period building overlooking a lush private garden square. Although the exterior of the building was ancient, the inside was a work of modern art. The diamond-patterned monochrome tiles from the steps outside continued into the entrance hall and reception area. There was a large kidney-shaped white stone counter in the centre that, along with the fresh bouquet of colourful flowers, housed two fashionable receptionists in their 20s. One had peroxide hair in a slick, blunt bob and the other had her chocolate tresses pulled back in a ponytail. They both wore red lipstick smothered across their probably botoxed lips and both were donning bright block colour summer dresses, the one with the bob in orange and the ponytailed one in cobalt blue. They both gave a flash of their veneered teeth and leapt up from their seats as soon as they saw Olivia arrive.

'Oh my God, babe!' cooed the blonde, air kissing Olivia as she walked over to the desk.

'How do you do it?' chimed in the brunette, in a whispery tone of admiration.

'Oh, I know, I know!' Olivia fanned her face with her hand as if she was a princess being fanned by a servant with a giant leaf.

The two girls and Olivia then gathered round one of the Apple computers and 'oohed' and 'ahhed' and giggled.

'Bay, have you not seen this yet?' Olivia called Bay over to the computer.

Bay wandered over and gave a shy wave to the two girls before leaning over the computer. And there, spread over the *Daily Mail* online site, were the four girls: Mia, Molly, Olivia and herself, heading into the club from last night. Bay grinned as she admired the way the flash of the paparazzi's cameras lit up her cheekbones and how every sequin on the dress she had been wearing twinkled like fairy lights. They looked like a girl band even if she did say so herself, if Little Mix were a little less edgy and The Spice Girls were more refined, a mix of *Gossip Girl* chic and *Sex and The City* glamour. Bay grinned as Olivia scrolled through the article. It was mostly focussed on Mia of course, and the other three girls had simply been described as 'and friends', but that was good enough for Bay. On her first evening out in London she'd made it to the home page of *Daily Mail* Online; her colleagues at home would be so jealous she had gone from writing articles to being in them! What could possibly happen next? she thought.

As Olivia carried on scrolling, Mia arrived in the reception. She gave the girls a weak smile and strode over. The two secretary girls returned to their seats as Mia passed the dresses from the night before to Olivia.

They too looked immaculate and Mia had even bothered to hang them up, unlike the women in the changing room at Zara who seem to discard their unwanted garments in a pile like they were punishing the clothes for not flattering them.

'Thanks, hun,' she said as Olivia inspected the dresses. 'Come on, Bay, the car's waiting.'

Bay followed Mia as she headed towards the Mercedes parked outside and clambered in. 'Not far to go,' Mia said, staring out of the tinted window which made the world look a lot darker.

'Do you feel prepared?' Bay asked, to try and lift the mood as Mia seemed rather quiet and not the bubbly, light up the room woman she met the day before.

'Yes and no,' Mia pondered. 'We'll only be given the script to learn when we arrive, so I don't really know what to expect,' she explained, as she flipped open a pocket mirror to check her lipstick.

'Oh, I see,' Bay paused. 'Great article in the Daily Mail!' she announced energetically. 'We looked amazing!'

'Are you fucking kidding? Yeah, we *looked* good, but did you read what they wrote about me?' Mia snapped the mirror shut.

Bay admitted to herself that in all the glory of her looking like a superstar in the article, she may have overlooked actually reading it. 'No, what did they say?' she asked, feeling a little like the wind had been knocked out of her sails.

'Only that I behaved like a spoilt brat crossed with a bunny boiler when I saw Max chatting to Amy. They even wrote that I can't handle the limelight and that my speedy rise to fame has resulted in me becoming arrogant and entitled. Onlookers were apparently shocked when I threw the entire table and its contents over Max. I mean, it's complete bullshit. As if I'd be able to pick up the table!' Mia let out a heavy sigh.

Bay thought Mia was probably worrying about the wrong part of the story and that maybe the 'arrogant' and 'entitled' part was a bit more career destroying than whether she did or didn't manage to pick up a table. 'So, who do you think gave them the info?'

'Who do you think? I'd bet my life on it being Amy! I can't believe she'd so publicly try to sabotage my career *and* before the audition. Archie is already trying to do damage control by reaching out to alcohol-free brands to collaborate with them.'

Then, just as they pulled up outside the industrial-looking warehouse in Battersea, they saw none other than Amy walking in.

'Are you fucking kidding me!' Mia's olive skin was beginning to turn red around her chest and face.

'Didn't you know she'd be here?' Bay was a bit confused.

'I thought there would be a high chance that she would be, but I really wanted to arrive before her.' Mia grabbed her phone and started tapping away furiously.

Bay could just about make out the message she was sending to Archie - 'Plan ruined'. It was then that Bay wondered if the perfectly put together Mia was really as perfect as she seemed. What was the plan and why was it ruined? Was it to do with Amy? So many thoughts crossed Bay's mind as they walked into the warehouse.

Another building whose outside facade was deceptive; inside it was refreshingly airy and cool with a huge glass roof allowing the sun to beat down on the greenhouse-style setting below. Exotic plants covered the open plan area making it smell like a rainforest; palm trees towered over the white metal seats and cacti stood tall in their terracotta pots dotted around the room. It looked more like a garden centre than an audition waiting room, but Bay guessed this was the kind of cool impression the artistic and creative types liked nowadays.

Mia was handed her script by a tall, skinny boy with glasses and curly, mousy brown hair. He was the epitome of an intern who was probably fresh out of drama school and buzzing about getting an unpaid role remotely in the sector he was attempting to pursue as a career. Mia and Bay then headed to one of the white metal tables. Amy was sat at another table just to the right of them studying her script and mouthing the words silently. She looked like a goldfish searching for food. The whole set up, bar the funky decor, was reminiscent of preparing for an exam and cramming in the final bits of revision before sitting the test.

'Right, I'm going to confront her about the article.' Mia got up from her chair before Bay could even say that this was neither the time nor the place to air their personal issues, for both their sakes. Although, this *was* where drama was being born, maybe the producers were looking for a bit of over the top confrontation. The conversation between the two seemed to get off to a smooth start; they were both smiling, and no one had attempted to take a swipe at the other!

'Girls!' the skinny boy's voice boomed surprisingly through the room.

Mia and Amy exchanged glances and walked towards him.

'I need you to sign these non-disclosure forms,' he said, thrusting a rather large wad of papers in front of them as if it contained NASA's top secrets.

Mia then waved at Bay and pointed at a piece of paper sat on the table Amy had been sat at. 'My script,' she mouthed at Bay.

Luckily, Bay was good at lip reading and scuttled over to retrieve the script lying on the table, before taking it back to where she was sitting. It was a good five minutes before Mia and Amy had signed the agreement, probably pretending to read the small print and Bay wished she had used the time to be nosey and read the script instead of jumping online to search for jobs. Mia and Amy then returned to their separate tables.

'My script!' yelled Amy, throwing her neck around to face Mia.

'Oh sorry, I must have picked it up.' Mia produced another script from her bag and returned it to Amy before Bay realised what had happened.

Mia and Amy were then called into another room and Bay was left sat in silence. She gasped when she realised what she'd just been a part of. Mia had asked her to collect the script from Amy's table, which Bay presumed was Mia's, left when she chatted to Amy. Well, Mia did say it was hers, when in fact it was Amy's. But when Amy had realised her script was missing Mia had given her another script from her bag. But what had been on the script Mia had given Amy? Had Bay just helped Mia sabotage Amy's audition?

The silence was broken by the audition room door bursting open and a tanned brunette running out in floods of angry tears, slamming the door behind her and nearly bowling over the skinny intern like a rugby player tackling the opposition.

'Mia!' Bay jumped to her feet to chase after her distraught friend, when Mia suddenly appeared out of the same door, shaking hands with an elderly man, who looked about 60, in a gangster-style pinstripe suit. Bay realised it must have been Amy running out crying; the two brunettes really did look identical, particularly from behind.

Mia said her goodbyes to the suit-clad man and danced towards Bay like a four-year-old in ballet class, showing off to a crowd of admiring parents.

'I think I've done it!' Mia threw her arms around Bay's neck.

'Oh my God, that's insane, Mia, amazing! I'm so pleased!' Bay hoped her enthusiastic delivery would mask the bittersweet feeling and guilt she was being overcome with. She couldn't stop thinking about Amy but decided to press Mia about the situation at a later stage in the day, maybe after a couple of celebratory alcoholic beverages had been consumed. Or maybe not, after the way Mia had behaved in the club on last night's rampage.

'Time to celebrate!' Mia threw her hands in the air once more, grabbed Bay's hand and they both joyfully ran out of the building, ignoring the intern who had his smartphone out, looking like he was about to ask for a selfie.

'Mia!' A man's voice came out of the exit of the building. It was Bachelor Ben again. Bay looked him up and down and realised why all the girls fell at his feet. When she had seen him in the club last night it was quite dark, and she hadn't appreciated his masculine beauty! He certainly was a rather handsome chap, wearing black jeans, a plain white T-shirt and a black leather jacket, although it was about 18 degrees outside. It made Bay sweat just looking at him - but that could have been because of how damn good looking he was and not the thought of wearing a leather jacket in the summer sun!

'Two seconds, hop in and I'll be back.' Mia gestured at the door of the car and ran over to Ben.

Bay was sure Mia was going to hug him, but she didn't. Bay watched the two as they strolled along the front of the warehouse building. They stopped at a corner and disappeared around the side and out of view.

The door of the building opened once more and the elderly man came out, looking around and waving a bit of paper. He moved in short jogging paces as quickly as his body would allow him, like an aged bear lolloping along. He paused breathlessly at the corner where Mia and Ben had been and looked around. He then stopped dead in his tracks like he had seen a ghost and ran even quicker back towards the entrance and back inside. No sooner had he done so, Mia and Ben reappeared, shook hands and Mia glided back towards the car in elegant antelope-style strides.

'Ben just invited us all to a party tonight,' Mia squealed with excitement as she closed the door of the car. 'Could this day get any better?'

Bay felt uneasy about people counting their chickens before they hatched.

Chapter 6

'Two can keep a secret if one
of them is deceased.'

Mia ecstatically called pretty much everyone in her phone book to tell them the good news, that she was 80% sure she'd got the role. The odds were good, but Bay thought all bets should be off until it was 100%. She guessed that was the beauty of a gamble, but she wasn't much of a gambler herself. She'd been to Vegas once and the closest she'd got to gambling was holding a hundred dollar bill, that she'd received when exchanging her pounds, and a setup picture making it look like she'd won it at a fruit machine. She appreciated Mia's positivity though, or was it pompousness? She wasn't sure.

They pulled up outside The Bluebird, a fancy King's Road hangout often ventured to by the cast of *Made in Chelsea*, which attracted the reality TV fans in their masses. It was quiet midweek and they opted for a table outside as the sun had showed its face again.

'Four please,' signalled Mia. Having called her agent with the positive news of destroying the competition, they had invited Archie and Molly to join them.

Although the eatery was on a main road, once you were seated, the thick green hedge absorbed the noise of car engines and impatient honks of the London drivers. The grey paving slabs of the outside terrace had been covered in sky-blue, Aztec patterned, weatherproof mats. The walls were painted white and the chairs had red, white and blue coloured cushions in various prints; spots, stripes and zig zags. It gave the place a coastal vibe which reminded Bay of home.

They were seated on a table at the back on a white bench with a long royal blue cushion on it, the kind you'd find on an old-fashioned garden bench swing. Bay enjoyed taking in the scenery as they sat down, whilst Mia tapped away on her phone. Growing up by the sea had given Bay the ability to appreciate a beautiful view. The outside barbeque area was lit and a cook, complete with white chef hat and navy and white striped apron, pushed burgers, sausages and Cajun-coated chicken thighs around on the griddle. As the meats sizzled, bursts of delicious smelling smoke drifted across the courtyard. Bay's stomach rumbled as she inhaled the fragrant air.

Mia looked up and giggled as she heard it. 'All right, I'll put my phone down and read the menu.' She laughed, silencing the phone and placing it on her side plate.

It had gone two o'clock and although Bay usually had a ham and cheese toastie around midday, she was realising Londoners did everything later. Breakfast meetings were at 9.30am, lunch at 2pm, dinner at 8pm after some tapas or light bites and sundowners at 5pm, clubs after 10.30pm and bed in the early hours of the next day. Tonight would be just that, after they had told Olivia the good news she insisted they meet at the White Horse after her shoot, for nibbles before heading to the rooftop party that Ben had invited them to later in the evening.

Finally, Mia had scouted the menu for what she fancied, a chicken Caesar salad without the chicken. Bay refrained from pointing out that was just a Caesar salad. As they were about to order, Archie and Molly arrived. Bay was now officially starving and the thought of having to wait another ten minutes for the couple to decide on food made her even more impatient. Another waiter passed, carrying a bright orange drink in a round bowl shaped glass, just the look of it quenched Bay's thirst.

'I want one of those!' she exclaimed, pointing towards the tray.

Mia raised her hand to her chest and patted it like she was saluting in the army. 'A girl after my own heart.' She smiled proudly like a parent whose child had just won a spelling bee.

'That, Bay, is an Aperol Spritz,' said Molly, raising her hand to summon a waiter. 'Aperol, which is a fruity liqueur, Prosecco and soda water.'

'Music to my Italian ears, we used to drink these in Positano every summer, they are an Italian celebratory cocktail, and this is just the occasion. Four Aperol Spritz please,' Mia chimed at the waitress before she'd even had time to get her notepad and pen out of her shirt breast pocket.

'And a burger.' Bay was quick to add, forcing Molly and Archie to make their food choice speedily.

The waitress was back in a flash carrying the cocktails, their coral hue glistening in the sun.

'Cheers to me!' laughed Mia raising her glass in the air.

'Cheers!' echoed Molly.

'Salut!' Bay remembered one of three Italian words she'd learnt. Mia was impressed and gave a big smile.

They all looked at Archie waiting for him to join the celebration and raise his glass. 'Look, I didn't want to ruin the party...' Archie began.

'Well, you are!' snapped Mia.

'Just because Amy ran out crying doesn't mean that *you've* definitely got the part. I'm just being realistic,' he pushed back.

'Oh, Archie, seriously, enough with the negativity recently. It sounds pretty horrific for Amy though, they can't possibly give her the role after that, it's so cringe!' Molly pulled a dramatic screwed up face to match her description.

'Yeah, what actually happened?' Bay mustered up the courage to ask Mia after her first sip of a rather strong Aperol Spritz.

Mia shot Bay a glance that simply read, *don't you dare say anything about what happened, or I won't be your friend anymore.* Just like back at primary school when you'd resist being a tattletale for the sake of a friendship and Bay was in no position to be losing friends.

Mia simply said, 'Oh, she read the completely wrong thing and the producers laughed. I think they thought it was actually funny, but you know how uptight Amy is, she took it so seriously.'

Bay wasn't entirely sure whether this was the truth or a lie but she daren't question further.

'Well, whatever happened, we can't start jumping for joy just yet.' Archie brought everyone back down to reality. 'Look, I know this is an odd request, but I think you should invite Amy tonight.'

Mia nearly spat out her Aperol Spritz. 'What. The. Fuck?' she said in slow syllables, a little too loudly. An older lady with a blue rinse turned around from the table behind and scowled at the group.

'Mia, I know it sounds ridiculous, but I promise it will make sense. It will be great for your reputation. Need I remind you of last night's hooha?' Sometimes Archie's words made Bay want to laugh. Even when he was being deadly serious, he'd always use the most hilarious words and in such a proper old English accent.

Bay could see Mia knew that her reputation was hanging by a thread by the way she eased her crumpled forehead to a more neutral tone, but her lips were still slightly pursed, looking like she was ready to argue back to whatever ridiculousness came out of Archie's mouth next.

'Just do it, Mia, and I'll take care of the rest!' Archie puffed, as if he was talking to a little disobedient puppy.

'Fine!' Mia reluctantly got out her phone and began typing. She read aloud and bobbed her head sarcastically from side to side as she put on a mocking voice. 'Dearest Amy, sorry that you fucked up royally today. Oh, please won't you join us to celebrate my success tonight so I can rub it in your face. Love Mia.' She looked at Archie, who wasn't entertaining her joke, and raised an eyebrow, just one, like the Rock used to do before a wrestling match. 'JK, just kidding, Archie!' She playfully ruffled his hair. She texted Amy a kinder, more sophisticated invite and everyone waited in anticipation of the reply.

An hour passed and they still hadn't heard anything. Suddenly Mia's phone pinged, and everyone jumped. Mia grabbed her phone.

'Urgh.' she moaned. 'It's only Olivia sending a voice note.' She clicked play and Olivia's voice rang out through the restaurant.

'Happy hump day, bitches! Just finished up, on my way to The Sloaney Pony - let's get this party staaaaaarted!'

Another message pinged in, and then another. Olivia was one of those people to send about ten short WhatsApp messages instead of just one long one. Mia clicked play again.

'I'll order ahead, what's everyone having? Tequila or Sambuca?'

The last message was Olivia cackling away to herself. As annoying and creepy as her laugh was, Bay was starting to enjoy its familiarity.

'Come on, let's go,' said Molly, downing the last droplets of her drink. People in London did not like to waste their alcohol.

The team arrived at the White Horse, a ten-minute Uber drive away, although if something wasn't within a 15-minute walking distance the locals would moan about commuting. Bay had heard that the average commute time to work in London was 52 minutes and as her group of new-found friends only seemed to commute from bar to bar in the same postcode she didn't think ten minutes was bad.

As Olivia had promised, she was at the last table in the sun, lapping up the last few rays as she sipped on a glass of such pale rosé it might as well be white.

'Darlings!' She stirred the air with her hand like the Queen, as she removed her stiletto courts from the black wrought iron railings they had been outstretched onto.

The girls joined the table whilst Archie headed to the bar. Typical Olivia had just organised a drink for herself despite her promises of shots, although Bay was relieved at the fact the night wouldn't be getting out of hand early on. Later on would be a different story, but for now things seemed like light-hearted fun. Mia's phone chimed again, and Bay and Molly peered at her with intent.

'No, it's not her!' Mia said shakily, almost blushing. Olivia saw her friend's flattered expression and grabbed the phone off Mia.

'What do we have here then, Missy?' she grinned.

Mia fought to get it back, but Olivia resisted, moving the phone to the other hand and almost elbowing Mia away.

'Bachelor Ben, hey. "Looking forward to seeing you later, told Carl you were coming and once he heard you'll be there he's insisted on joining too xx." Two Xs, hmm. Who's Carl?' she quizzed.

'Carl Baker!' Mia and Bay yelled the director's name at the same time.

'I should have introduced you today, Bay. Sorry it was all so overwhelming,' Mia apologised.

'He was there? Oh my God! I was in the same building as Carl Baker,' swooned Bay.

'Yeah, in the pinstripe suit,' replied Mia.

'No way, Mr Mafia was Carl Baker?' Bay said, knowing she'd not just been in the same building but inches away; he looked older in real life.

'Mr Mafia,' giggled Mia.

'Kind of fitting though,' Molly butted in. Bay looked blankly at her.

'Oh, please, Mol, that's just a rumour!' Mia shook her head, though not very convincingly.

'Explain, please!' Olivia sat bolt upright in her seat as Archie returned and handed out the rest of the drinks. Olivia loved to hear a bit of gossip, almost more than she loved clothes.

'Ages ago, a girl drowned in a pool at a party that was apparently at a venue Carl had ties to, although it was never proved that he owned it, or even had anything to do with it and he wasn't even there when it happened – it was all very hush hush. So that's about all we know.' Archie had arrived just in time to tell the story.

'Oh, boring!' Clearly the story wasn't at a level of scandal that Olivia turned her attention on for. Although it was a far more dramatic story than Bay had ever come across her desk in Cornwall.

Mia's phone pinged once more and again everyone took a sharp breath waiting to hear if it was Amy.

'Ben again. Saying cars are coming to Olivia's at six,' Mia said, looking at her watch. It was already 5.15 pm so they needed to drink up quickly.

'So, what happened with Amy's script then?' Olivia fished for more gossip, unsatisfied by the previous tale.

'Oh, she just messed it up,' shrugged Mia.

'But how? She's done auditions before, she can read. What did she mess up?' Olivia questioned.

'Don't know, Liv, she just read the wrong thing.' Mia's voice got louder.

'How did she read the wrong thing, was she given the wrong script?' Olivia persisted.

'I don't know, Olivia.' Mia's tone was harsh.

'Did you see anything?' Olivia fished for more information from Bay.

Mia shot Bay the same threatening glance she had earlier. Bay shook her head and curved her lips downwards to shrug off the question. She guessed she was taking this one to the grave.

CHAPTER 7

'A little party never killed anybody!'

A nother day, another unnecessary Uber, thought
Bay as they bumbled through the London streets.
They passed flashy parked cars: Porsches,
Ferraris and Maseratis left on the side of narrow roads
whilst their drivers, usually under the age of 35, would
pop into the many luxurious restaurants to sample
the cocktails, leaving two hours later with a female
companion and DUI waiting to happen. The cars told
Bay they were in Mayfair, and close to the party venue.

It was a 'white' party, which Bay had heard of once in
an episode of *The Kardashians* where everyone wears
white. Olivia had provided the outfits again. A halter
neck A-line shift dress for herself with silver chains
acting as a built-in necklace at the top. Such a dress
on Bay would probably make her look like she was
expecting but on Olivia with her height and long, slim
legs, it hung like a pretty vine wrapping itself around
all the right places. For Bay, Olivia had chosen a French
Connection bandage bodycon dress. It really flattered

her stomach and hips and with the Wonderbra Olivia had lent her, her assets were looking rather perky, too. Molly was in a pleated maxi dress which made her skin glow. It tied at the waist with a gold chain belt and she looked every inch the toga princess. As for Mia, well, of course she had the standout outfit of the evening. A backless white jumpsuit with long sleeves and a high neck holding the whole thing up. There was no need to accessorize a garment like that, Olivia had said, it needed no fuss and was striking enough on its own.

They exited the cab to more flashes of photographers' cameras outside. Although it was only the second time Bay had been papped, she was already taking to it like a duck to water, having watched the other girls the night before. This time she was more composed and less 'rabbit in the headlights' as she changed poses between flashes. There was a red carpet lined by a large manmade wall covered in logos of famous brands from Ralph Lauren to Ribena.

'Press Wall,' called Olivia, going into combat PR mode as she took her phone out of her oyster shell clutch whilst Mia queued up behind other semi well-known actors, musicians and influencers. When it was Mia's turn, Olivia started filming on her phone, following Mia's brunette hair as she flicked it from side to side.

'Mia, over here,' 'To the left sweetheart,' 'Looking fab Mia, face this way,' called the photographers vying for the best shot to send to their glossy magazines.

Bachelor Ben joined the queue of nearly-somebodies and Mia gave a little wave. The photographers clocked the interaction and called Ben through so they could be photographed together. They played to the wall of paparazzi, laughing, flashing their teeth and Ben even tucked an arm around Mia. It was just what the photographers wanted to see as the clicking of cameras got quicker. Mia looked slightly uneasy as she politely brushed off Ben's arm and waved goodbye to the media circus as she trotted off the carpet. Met by Olivia and the girls she exhaled a large amount of air.

'However much I do that, I'll never get used to it,' said Mia in a flurry. 'Did I look OK? Was my hair neat? Did I smile too much, not enough?' Bay couldn't quite decide if Mia's nerves and anxiety were getting to her again or if she was fishing for attention.

'Pretty as a picture,' Olivia instantly replied, like a robot who had clearly dealt with this before. She turned her back, grabbed a bubbling Prosecco from a waitress waiting at the foot of the steps and began ascending them. The others quickly followed their Queen Bee, each whipping a glass from the tray with a speedy, 'Thank you.'

The event was on the rooftop of one of the hotels that overlooked Berkley Square. They got to the lobby and crammed into a lift with a few other stragglers, up to the eighth floor. There weren't many massively tall buildings in Mayfair, so the view was spectacular from the atrium they exited into from the lift. It was all glass and allowed a 360-degree view of the city, from the Eye over to St Paul's and round to the BT Tower. Bay was pretty sure she could also make out Wembley's coloured halo to the west of Hyde Park. She took a moment to let it all in, it was like something out of a movie, the City lights twinkling away trying to outshine each other. She now understood why Londoners were so proud of their City and she felt proud of herself for making the decision to make the move here.

The atrium was filled with people all in white, some vying for attention in cream. There were maxi dresses, one pieces, flared trousers, suits, short shorts and mini dresses and everyone looked so glamorous against the shimmering backdrop of lights from central London at night.

The wait staff and barmen were also in white, making it all that bit more confusing as they wound their way through the obstacle course of people, offering up little snacks.

'Ooo, mini slider, don't mind if I do.' Olivia clutched at one of the perfectly round buns filled with a teeny tiny meat patty, one single lettuce leaf and a quarter of a tomato slice. She was like a child trying to fish out of a rockpool on a Cornish beach cove. Any food item that passed, Olivia was on to it – melba toast topped with salmon and cream cheese, a miniature mug of tomato soup and a peanut chicken skewer. At one point, Bay had to offer to hold Olivia's drink as she was running out of hand space to gather up her grazing goods.

'It's like you've just come out of hibernation and haven't seen food in the last six months,' joked Bay.

'Sweetie, when you've attended as many events as I have you quickly learn that these bites of heaven disappear quicker than you can say 'paparazzi'. I mean, just look at that oaf over there,' she said between mouthfuls of satay chicken, pointing to a man holding a stack of three mini burgers that he was about to devour.

Bay laughed; the sliders did look delicious. She caught the attention of a waiter and elegantly pincered one off the tray, like a crab, and popped it in her mouth. Olivia was right, they were little bites of heaven; the brioche bun melted in her mouth, its sweetness complimenting the slightly salted meat. There was neither too much nor too little salad as was often the case in a burger; the lettuce was crisp and the tomato fresh. And just like that it was gone.

The glass atrium led out onto a selection of balconies and roof terraces, and as the girls made their way through the crowds, they bumped into many familiar faces. Max and Archie had arrived and were dressed in matching cream linen suits. Archie with a pink striped shirt and pink pocket square and Max in the same but in blue. They looked like two pageboys dressed up for a photo-shoot for the Little White Company. Mia had excused herself to chat briefly to Bachelor Ben, and Carl Baker, who Bay instantly recognised from the audition earlier. He now looked very Grecian in his white tailored trousers and cream jacket.

After mingling with everyone, they finally found a deserted balcony covered with flower walls overlooking a residential courtyard eight floors below. Despite it being nearly 7pm, this little balcony was still in the sun and the girls sat down at a stone table with matching stone benches to watch the sunset. The glass balustrade glowed as the sun made its descent. It was peaceful out on the balcony despite the flurry of people inside, buzzing around greeting each other like busy bees collecting pollen. Instead of pollen, the socialites were gathering gossip and exchanging secrets.

Bay caught Carl Baker side-eyeing them every now and then and thought he must be discussing the film with Bachelor Ben by his side. Bachelor Ben's fiancé had arrived and was also eyeing up Mia, although her gaze was more like that of a green-eyed monster. She was older but still oozed glamour, wearing a midi ruched skirt with matching crumpled boob tube in a thick fabric. She had very short brunette hair cut like the classic picture of Audrey Hepburn sat at a table with her cigarette. She had finished off her ensemble with a bold red lip colour. Her name was Kristen and she was a writer for various comical TV series, although her face, at this time, did not show an ounce of humour. No-one had thrown this much shade since the Cardi B/Nicki Minaj fiasco.

Just as it seemed the girls would be able to spend the evening in peace on the balcony, an unexpected arrival appeared through the soundproofed glass doors. It was Amy, dressed in flared white trousers and a low-back, high neck top with long sleeves, almost identical to Mia's outfit. Her brown hair was pulled up in a scruffy bun and she had wisps of stray baby hairs framing her face. Mia looked up and her face dropped.

'Girls, can you give us a minute please?' she asked politely, ushering Molly, Bay and Olivia up off their benches.

Olivia looked most put out and the frown didn't lift from her face until they'd gone back inside and reached the bar. After receiving a Mimosa, Olivia's icy expression melted away, thawed by the liquid intake.

'What do you think they are talking about?' asked Molly, sipping from her blue iced cocktail.

'Saving the world, figuring out Brexit... I don't know, Molly – Maybe the mystery of the script at the audition today? That drink has gone to your head, what the hell is it? It looks like a blue WKD has shat in it.' Olivia let out another of her cackles and Molly joined in.

They continued to watch Mia and Amy on the balcony, both stood by the glass balustrade, their forearms resting on the top. Amy tugged at her topknot until the hair tie snapped and her long brown hair cascaded down her back like in a L'Oreal advert. They now looked identical in their low backed outfits with their long dark hair and caramel complexions. They didn't appear to be arguing, although there was a lot of waving of hands and hair flicks which Bay thought was a good sign. At least they weren't trying to throw each other over the edge.

Suddenly, there was a loud gong, followed by a fancy announcement inviting everyone into the Mayfair Suite to listen to a speech about a charity. The crowds pushed each other frantically in a stampede, as if there was free money being handed out. The crowd went back towards the lifts to a meeting room on the other side, bottlenecking at the door like a herd of sheep trying to squeeze their fluffy, off-white bodies through a gate. The girls looked back at Mia and Amy who were still on the balcony.

'They probably haven't heard through the doors, should I get them?' asked Molly.

'Don't be ridiculous, and miss our next free tipple? How many times do I need to remind you, free stuff disappears fast around here?' sighed Olivia pointing towards a diminishing tray of Prosecco at the doorway. On command the three of them strutted over, claiming their glasses of bubbly before entering the meeting room.

It really wasn't large enough to contain this number of people and they were all crammed into any spare crevices like you do when getting on the central line at rush hour, except the men here sweated out Yves St Laurent instead of, well, actual sweat. It was so cramped that even if they had spotted Archie and Max, they wouldn't have been able to reach them. The girls took up position just inside the door and Molly suddenly elbowed Olivia.

'Ouch.' Olivia elbowed back. 'What was that for?'

'It's Max's dad, ssh!' whispered Molly, signalling towards the just-about-visible stage with her eyes.

Max's dad was just like Max, a preppy Ken Doll, rather fetching for a guy who was nearing 60. He made a brief speech before introducing a lanky man with an iPad to the stage to talk about the charity they were all there to support. Max's dad snuck out swiftly through another door at the back of the room which, presumably, went back to the atrium and he closed the door as quietly as possible as if not to be noticed.

Then the door the girls had come through burst open, banging into Olivia's leg.

'For fuck's sake!' she yelled too loudly at the perpetrator behind the door. It was Archie.

'Where have you been all night?' Molly reached over to try to kiss her boyfriend but couldn't quite stretch that far and caught Olivia's arm with her mouth instead. Olivia brushed off the clammy lip gloss like a bug had just landed on her and needed removing immediately.

'I had to take care of something,' he replied with a smile.

The man on the stage droned on for a few minutes before the door flung open onto Olivia for a second time.

'Seriously!' she boomed.

But even Olivia's voice was drowned out by the loud, hysterical screams of the waitress who had entered. She was barely able to stand, let alone talk, and her face was red, tearstained and screwed up like a new-born baby.

'What's happened?' Archie managed to steady the woman as she staggered into the room and the place fell silent.

She could only point to the atrium as the room all turned at once to see. Some other staff members had heard the commotion and were running around the atrium trying to locate the source of the screaming.

'Rosa, what is it?' A smartly dressed boy in his late 20s comforted the waitress as he attempted to escort her out of the room back towards the atrium. His tag said 'Sam, Events Manager'.

'Sam, quick, the balcony!' Another young waitress called to the Events Manager from the other side of the glass walled atrium, her voice echoing in the silence.

'A girl's fallen!' The second waitress also began sobbing uncontrollably. 'She's down there, oh God, all I could see was her beautiful brown hair among the bushes below.'

Bay was sure her heart stopped for a second. Her throat suddenly felt dry and yet her hands were clammy with perspiration. It seemed like the world stood still for a minute until the silence was broken and the sounds of panicked voices, hushed whispers and distant sirens filled her ears, making her dizzy.

'Oh My God, Mia!' Molly looked at the group, her face whiter than normal.

CHAPTER 8

'Once you're dead, you're made for life.' – Jimi Hendrix

As the girls all stood in panic, eight stories up in the hotel atrium, Bay realised the night had all been a bit of a blur to her. She didn't know if it was the excitement of being at one of London's elite parties or the amount of free alcohol she had consumed. She would be useless in a police line-up, she thought, barely even remembering the name of the hotel they were at. Bay swallowed hard as the reality hit her that she might indeed be involved in a police line-up.

Molly was in tears, huddled under Archie's arm. Each tear that dripped off her heavy mascara-clad eyelashes making a smudged grey mark on Archie's once-pristine suit jacket.

Many of the other guests were weeping as the confusion and shock of the situation sunk in. Some had chosen to leave and a queue for the lifts was forming. Others were hanging around to try and find out exactly what was going on and this gaggle of people were currently being held back by a small team of three security guards with their arms outstretched making a human chain separating the punters from the scene. Their walkie-talkies crackled continuously with people muttering numbers and something about balconies.

The lift suddenly pinged making everyone jump and a group of about eight police officers got out. The second lift did the same and out spilled more officers, like ants who had just had their nest disturbed. Sam, the Events Manager guy, rushed over and shook hands with what Bay assumed was the Chief Officer in charge but the girls were too far away to hear any of the conversation and Bay's lip reading skills were seriously clouded by her brain desperately trying to sober up.

Suddenly Olivia ducked under the security guards' arms, causing one of them to chase after her.

'Touch me and I'll sue you,' she said calmly but confidently, and the guard stopped in his tracks and lowered his arms.

'You can't be here,' he said, ushering Olivia back towards the crowd of people like a sheepdog.

The party of onlookers began demanding answers and started yelling questions 'What's happened?', 'Tell us what's going on!', 'Has somebody fallen?', 'Are they dead?'

'Get these people out of here,' ordered the Chief Policeman and the security guards began pushing their human daisy chain towards the lifts.

'You will let me through, you pesky little man!' Olivia was still battling with the guard who became more obstructive the angrier she got.

Bay, seeing that Olivia was getting nowhere with her aggressive attitude, realised she needed to approach the situation with a different attitude. 'Sir, we think it's our friend,' she said quietly but with enough passion to grab the attention she needed.

The Chief turned to look at them, Molly's still-damp face assisting with applying some pressure.

'Come with me.' He led the girls towards the balcony and Bay called Olivia over, who, released from the Guard's grip, smoothed down her dress and cantered over to join them.

'I'll leave you to it,' Archie said passing Molly over to Bay.

'What?' blubbered Molly

'It's fine, call me when you're done.' And with that, he scampered off.

The officer sat them down at a table whilst the police cordoned off the area with blue and white striped tape. The noise from the other partygoers had eased as the lifts took groups of the people down and out into the cool of the night.

'A girl has fallen from the balcony here; we can't tell you more than that simply because we don't know any more ourselves. Was this where you last saw your friend?' he asked gently.

'Is she dead?' Olivia answered his question with another question.

'I can neither confirm nor deny that I'm afraid. Now can you describe your friend please, what's her name?'

'Mia Bonaventura,' mumbled Molly, who had begun crying again.

'She's wearing a white Dolce and Gabbana jumpsuit, it's high necked and backless,' Olivia described the designer outfit with a little more detail than was probably necessary. 'With long sleeves,' she added, her voice wobbling.

The officer's face had 'no idea how to spell Dolce and Gabbana' written all over it as he took notes on a pathetically small notepad. Realising that he needed more information other than just what and who she was wearing, Bay took the reins again.

'She's got long brown hair, olive skin and she's about five-ten.'

The officer paused this time, he called over a colleague and they began whispering, 'Olive skin, long brown hair, backless outfit'. His colleague nodded and rushed off.

'All right, thank you, girls. I think you'd better go now. I can't say any more until we've established identity and informed next of kin.' The officer folded his little notepad and popped it back into his jacket.

'So, she is dead!' Molly burst into tears once more and Olivia and Bay put an arm each around her whilst heading solemnly towards the lift. It arrived almost immediately, and they shuffled in, dragging their once sprightly stiletto heels behind them. Molly was beginning to remove hers altogether. Olivia slumped heavily against the mirror in the elevator and Bay could tell she was holding back tears as Olivia averted her eyes when

Bay looked at her. The elevator stopped at the third floor and the girls quickly tried to compose themselves as best they could under the tragic circumstances.

The doors slowly rolled open to a sight that nearly knocked them all to the floor – it was Mia, as large as life. Bay was speechless, a mix of confusion and relief ran through her like someone had just switched on a kettle and it was beginning to bubble.

'What the actual fuck!' Olivia grabbed her friend by the neck of the Dolce and Gabbana number she had recently so intricately described and dragged her by the collar into the lift.

'Whoa! What's going on? How many tequilas have you had?' Mia laughed whilst looking Molly, shoes in hand, up and down.

'What's going on? You're dead!' boomed Olivia, but they reached the ground floor and the doors opened once again before any explanation could be made.

'Oh!' exclaimed Mia, looking at the two men in front of her. It was Bachelor Ben and Carl Baker, and both looked at Mia in shock.

'Ladies,' said Ben, wedging his hand in the doors so they didn't start to shut again. He awkwardly raised his other arm halfway up like an air hostess pointing out the exit routes on an aeroplane.

'Thanks.' Mia brushed past and led the girls out.

'Where are they going and why are they going back in?' asked Molly.

'Probably heading back to the party. Anyway, where the hell are we going, the party is that way and what's this about me being dead..?' Mia stopped in her tracks as she saw the blue flashing lights of several police cars and ambulances. She paused before the glass door of the lobby to assess the scene. There were armed police, news teams and their branded vans, presenters with microphones and people dressed in white overalls and hoods carrying tents.

'What's going on? What's happened?' she asked, her voice turning shrill with panic. Olivia pulled Mia once more, this time by the arm, behind a marble pillar. Molly threw her arms around Mia, who patted her back.

'Someone has fallen off the balcony and we thought it was you,' Olivia explained.

'Oh my God!' Mia raised one hand to her mouth and hugged Molly a little tighter with the other. 'And you thought it was me?' She lowered her hand from her mouth to her chest. 'You guys.' She gathered up Bay and Olivia into a group hug.

Olivia pulled away, with bits of Mia's hair that had got stuck to her lip gloss in the tight embrace.

'If you didn't fall, who did?' she asked.

'I don't know. I had a successful conversation with Amy and then I left to go to the bathroom and when I came out, you'd all disappeared.'

Bay inhaled quickly putting two and two together. 'Amy!' she whispered.

Trying to avoid the media frenzy outside, the girls skirted the hotel lobby for another exit. There was a door just before the restaurant marked 'bins' so, after checking no-one was looking, they pushed it open. Sure enough, the rundown corridor turned a corner and led to another door with a push barrier. They pushed it open and entered the night air on to a back alley in Mayfair where they could still hear the ear-piercing sounds of the sirens.

'Let's get a cab back to yours, Liv,' Mia suggested, heading towards a busier road.

'On it,' Olivia replied, tapping on her phone. 'Three minutes.'

'I'm just going to call Archie to let him know that we're OK,' Molly said, stepping aside.

The other three huddled around a post-box and silently took in the events of the evening.

'Guys,' Molly came rushing over. She held out her phone which was on speaker. 'Archie is with Max and Max's dad'.

'Hi, girls!' Max's voice came through the phone. 'We're in the bar on the ground floor. Hope everyone's OK. Do you want to join us?'

'No. It's OK, babe, we're gonna go to Liv's,' replied Mia.

'OK. God what an evening. Poor Amy,' he said, sadly.

'So, it was definitely her?' Mia asked, sighing. 'How do you know?'

'Dad said it was her,' replied Max.

'How does he know? There's nothing online yet.' Mia scrolled through her phone on a news app.

'Dunno how he knows, but that's what he said.'

The taxi home seemed to take forever, maybe because all of their minds were on the events of the evening or because Bay so desperately wanted to be back in a safe and familiar place. Even though she had only been in London for a few days, Olivia's little flat was starting to feel like a home from home. Bay glanced around the taxi, appreciating the friends she sat there with and that she didn't have to go through the night's events alone. She felt a pang of guilt run through her that it had taken such a devastating event to make her thankful for the company of others.

They arrived back at Olivia's flat where the kettle was soon being boiled and Olivia was deciding which aperitif to add to the hot chocolate she was making. Everyone was still very quiet, only murmuring a 'thank you,' when Olivia brought over the whipped-cream-topped hot chocolates and a plate of rich tea biscuits.

'I guess we'd better see what's going on, then.' Olivia aimed the remote at the telly and changed the channel from MTV's Greatest Hits to Sky news and there it was, the confirmation they had been dreading. The red banner flashed at the bottom 'Partygoer who fell from rooftop of Mayfair Hotel is pronounced dead at the scene'.

CHAPTER 9

'Did she fall, or did she jump?'

The girls slept in the lounge, apart from Olivia who had headed to the comfort of her own bed. Bay didn't sleep well at all and waking up was like coming round from one of those dreams when you didn't know whether it was real or not. Unfortunately, the fate of Amy was only too horribly true. Mia's phone hadn't stopped ringing since about 6am and it appeared she'd now turned it off altogether. Clearly, people had found out that she was possibly the last person to see Amy alive.

'Girls!' Olivia ran into the lounge, attempting to tie her white towel robe with one hand whilst balancing her Mac Book in the other. 'Look at this,' she said, holding out the laptop.

'What does it say?' asked Molly, rushing over from the kitchen where she had been rummaging about for breakfast. She squeezed onto the sofa next to Olivia, who wiggled the laptop mouse around until the page lit up. It was the Sun Online and Molly read aloud. '"Did she fall, or did she jump?" That's the headline, then it says "Did Amy Braybury jump off the balcony after finding out she'd lost out on the lead role in *The Trouble With Us* to pal Mia Bonaventura. Was this literally the final tipping point for her?"' The girls all looked at Mia for an answer.

'OK, all right. Carl told me at the audition that I had definitely got the role but I haven't signed the contract yet, so I didn't want to blab and it all get out before it was official,' Mia explained.

'Do you think she'd actually jump, though? Because of that? Did she even know?' quizzed Molly, reading the article again.

'No. How could she have known? And even if she did, I really don't think she'd do that. She's too well set up at home with her dad's money and it's not like her life depended on this job,' Mia argued.

'Well, it kind of did, the poor bitch is dead now.' Olivia got up from her seat and headed to the kitchen. 'Coffee, anyone? I take it no one's off to work then.' The Nespresso machine whirred into action.

Molly shook her head as if responding to Olivia, although she didn't even have a job to call in and say she wasn't going to. She seemed to be the most shaken about the events.

'Yep, you've convinced me.' Olivia held her phone to her ear and recorded a nonchalant message to her office about a client needing to see her and how she wouldn't be in today.

'I don't have any plans today,' followed Mia, 'and Bay doesn't even have a job, so...'

Bay gave a little laugh as she remembered why she had come to London. Her laughter soon faded as she realised for the first time the sheer horror that someone had died at a party she had attended. Was she even more involved than simply being in the same room as Amy? She had, after all, been involved in the sabotage of Amy's audition. By accident or not, she still played a part. Had that been the beginning of poor Amy's downfall? She tried to ignore the headlines. She knew all too well that journalists were unfortunately always making headlines with reports of celebrities over-dosing, putting bullets in their heads and even jumping off hotel balconies.

'How did she seem when you were chatting to her?' Bay asked Mia, fishing for some more information on the conversation.

'She sounded fine, she wasn't drunk, she wasn't angry, she was just polite and listened,' Mia replied.

Molly's phone rang. It was Archie. 'Good news,' he said, not a note of sympathy or sadness in his voice. 'Tell Mia the contract is here and I'm sending it over to sign now. Oh, and tell her to put her phone back on, I feel it's going to be a busy day.'

Clearly everyone is just carrying on with business as usual, thought Bay, and maybe she should too.

'Liv, can I borrow your printer?' Mia called, battling with the sound of the coffee machine.

'Prosecco, sure sweetie, it's in the fridge but if you want the Verve it's in the cupboard,' Olivia called, popping her head up at the mention of booze.

'No, *printer*, although now I've got the contract through, I guess we could celebrate with a glass.'

'Printer, hah! I haven't had one since 2012. The only thing starting with a 'P' here is Prosecco,' Olivia was already unwrapping the top of the bottle.

'Oh well, I'll print it at Max's later, I've got to go and get some things from his, anyway.' Mia reached for her phone and turned it on again, then joined the girls in the kitchen. Olivia had poured four glasses of fizz and topped them up with a dash of orange juice. She pushed a glass towards each of the other three girls.

'I'd just like to say ...' Olivia began a speech before she was cut off by the bleeping of Mia's phone.

'Ignore it, continue, Liv,' Mia said, rolling her eyes in the direction of her phone.

'We are so proud of you and ...' Olivia was cut short by another ringing of the phone. 'Oh, bloody cheers!' she finished, not attempting the speech for a third time and clinked glasses before taking a big swig.

'Urgh, I'd better see what it is.' Mia reluctantly made her way towards her phone whilst Bay searched Olivia's cupboards for anything edible and non-alcoholic.

'It's like a bar in here, Liv. When do you ever drink this?' asked Bay, holding up a matte black bottle with a picture of a sunset on it.

'All the time, Passoa is delicious!' Olivia grabbed the bottle and poured a little drop into each glass.

'Are you sure it's still in date? The bottle is very dusty,' Molly quizzed returning the sticky bottle to the cupboard.

'Yes, of course, it's alcohol. It never goes off!' Olivia adamantly replied.

'Shit, *shit!*' exclaimed Mia from the sofa.

'Shit what?' asked Olivia, rushing over then rushing back to the kitchen to retrieve her forgotten glass before darting back to the sofa again.

'I've got a missed call from the police. They want to talk to me as they know I was with her.' Mia looked really panicked. 'What do I do?'

Olivia peeled the phone from Mia's hand to listen to the message.

'Standard procedure, it sounds like. They just want to find out details of her final movements,' Olivia explained, like she was on CSI. 'Call them back and arrange a chat. I think they've left a text too.'

Olivia was about to open Mia's inbox when Mia yanked the phone back out of Olivia's hands with such force it nearly flew across the room.

Mia read the message, it was from Archie. 'The police called and want to talk to you. I'm coming round so we can prep.'

'What is there to prep? This isn't an interview in Vogue, surely you just tell them what you know?' Olivia stirred her drink with her finger until the liquid blended into an orange colour. She had a point, thought Bay. What was there to 'prep' for a police questioning?

Mia had put her phone down and was now gazing out of the window awaiting Archie's arrival. Bay didn't like the atmosphere one bit; the usually loud bunch of girls were quiet and sitting apart from one another. The tight-knit group she had got so much warmth from in the taxi last night was shattered into the various corners of Olivia's flat. Eventually, Archie's taxi pulled up outside and he was buzzed in the main door. He kissed Molly quickly on the forehead before laying his laptop, a camera and a notepad out on the kitchen worktop.

'Right, we need to work out timings, what was said, why there's a rift between you two and why she might have chucked herself off the balcony,' he said, bluntly, as he began setting up his video camera.

'What are you doing with that?' Mia asked, looking into the camera lens like it was a natural reaction.

'We've got to see where you stumble in your questioning and what you have trouble remembering,' he replied, fiddling with a USB cable and unplugging Olivia's NutriBullet blender to accommodate his charger.

'Archie, it's not a murder enquiry,' snorted Olivia into another drink she'd made herself sometime during the morning. 'I think she can handle the popo's enquiries. This isn't *Line of Duty* although I wish it was – who saw the finale? Brutal!' It was typical of Olivia to always switch a serious topic to a lighter theme around TV shows and celeb gossip, thought Bay. Half of her thought it distasteful and rude but on the other hand it made her thankful some joviality had returned to the room.

'Yes, but we need to get things right! Now, what will you say when they ask where you were around 8pm last night?' Archie got behind his laptop, ready to type, and positioned the camera onto Mia's face.

'I was at the hotel, I don't remember where, I was looking for the girls,' she responded with a shrug.

'No. There should be no not remembering, Miss Bonaventura. You need to be 110% clear. You say, "I was in the atrium with Archie looking for my friends."' He looked Mia dead in the eye.

Bay hated the phrase '110%' or any percent over 100 as it is literally impossible to give more than 100%. It even annoyed her on programmes, such as *X-Factor* when the judges say 'wow, you really gave it 120%'. She also didn't like the way Archie had become so pushy.

'But, Archie, I wasn't with you.' Mia frowned.

'Yes, I know, but if you weren't with anyone then if we say we were together, I can back you up as an alibi,' he huffed.

'But Archie, that's a lie.' Molly tilted her head like a puppy that is trying to understand the baby chatter talked to it by cooing humans.

'Oh, Molly, please, we've been over this. Sometimes you have to work in the grey, sweetheart,' he reasoned impatiently with his girlfriend.

'She's right though, Archie. What if they find out it's a lie?' Mia defended her friend.

'Will you please stop using the word *lie*, this is not a lie. You're all blowing things way out of proportion. Please just leave me to do my job - which is currently damage controlling this mess.' Archie's pale face turned redder and redder and he loosened his top shirt button and pulled at his collar to allow some airflow to his neck.

'Now, Mia, will you please sign that contract ASAP, before this thing all falls apart completely. I've stuck my neck out so much for you, now it's time you returned the favour. Get this interview out of the way and sign the freaking contract that I've worked so hard to get you.' Archie was beginning to sweat as he tugged harder at his shirt collar, as if he was somehow magically going to create a wind tunnel to his face.

Bay didn't know which she was most shocked by, Archie advising Mia to lie or Archie dripping in sweat, red faced and twitching slightly, like he was going to explode. She didn't trust him at all, and she watched as the other girls all fell silent except, surprisingly, Molly who had been burying her head in her phone and now bleated, 'Umm, guys...'

'Oh, for God's sake, what now, Mol?' Archie was nearly bursting at the seams.

Molly rushed to the TV remote and changed the channel again from some music to the news as the presenter began to speak. 'We have breaking news from London. The girl that plummeted eight stories from a hotel balcony has been confirmed as Amy Braybury, daughter of property developer Richard Braybury. The hotel has also confirmed they have released CCTV footage of the evening that is being reviewed by the police and this is now being treated as homicide.'

CHAPTER 10

**'Things always show up when
you're not looking for them.'**

'What does it mean?' Molly was furiously typing 'homicide' into a phone to get a definition. 'Murder?' she gasped.

'It means they don't have a clue!' Archie blurted out. He looked like he might keel over at any minute.

If Bay wasn't filled with panic before, she certainly was now! The situation had gone from accident to suicide to murder within hours and with each new revelation she had to adjust her thoughts accordingly, like it was happening over and over again. She felt slightly relieved that Amy hadn't done this to herself after losing out on the film role, but very much terrified that a murderer could have been within inches of her at the party. Maybe she had even spoken with them! Within minutes of the news breaking, Mia's phone rang again.

'It's the police,' she said, fear in her eyes.

'Answer it and explain everything,' Olivia said, with a hint of frustration in her voice.

'And remember what I said!' added Archie.

Mia took the call and headed to the hallway out of the prying ears of the others. She returned less than a minute later.

'Well?' Archie was the first to say anything.

'They want to see me today at 5pm.' Mia shrugged.

'That's fine, sweetie, don't worry about it. You've done nothing wrong so just tell the truth.' Olivia aimed the last bit of her sentence towards Archie.

'Tell them whatever you like, Mia, but have that contract signed and back to me before you do. I mean it.' Archie got up and headed for the door, already rolling a cigarette. 'See you later.' And with that he left, shutting the door behind him.

'What the hell is up with him? No offence, Mol, but he was being most peculiar.' Olivia looked at Molly.

'I'm just as baffled as you, Liv. Maybe he thinks the film will be cancelled after all of this drama. It's been going on for a few days now, all on edge and snappy.' Molly tried to make sense of her boyfriend's erratic behaviour.

Mia shuffled in her seat and bit her lip nervously. 'You don't think that Carl would stop the film, do you?' she asked.

'Better get that contract signed before anyone can change their mind. Make sure it's got a no filming or no release clause in it.' Olivia was back in PR mode again.

'A what clause?' questioned Bay.

'So that you still get paid a percentage if they cancel production during filming or if you've filmed everything and then it's pulled before release,' explained Olivia.

'I'll let Archie look at it all. I better get going. Oh damn, the District Line is down between Earls Court and Wimbledon!' Mia sighed as she read the TFL updates on her phone.

'Story of my life,' huffed Olivia.

'At least then I don't have to be seen in public looking like this.' Mia pointed to her bare, make-up free face which still looked better than Bay's fully caked face, Bay thought.

'Uber can be here in three,' Olivia pointed out.

'I know, but what if the driver recognised me and started asking questions after last night? It's probably all anyone in London is talking about!'

'Where are you going to? I can drive you if you like,' offered Bay, wanting to be useful.

'Oh Bay, you superstar, that would be amazing! Only to Victoria, it should take like 20 minutes.' Mia was already scooping up her bits into her clutch bag from the night before. She was dressed in the clothes she'd worn at the audition yesterday, before they had changed at Olivia's for the white party.

'Good luck with the interview, talk to you later,' Molly said sweetly from the lounge as Bay and Mia left. Olivia simply lifted a hand as she was fully ensconced in an article from this week's Vogue.

It did only take about 20 minutes to drive along the King's Road, all the way past Sloane Square and into

Eaton Square, one of Belgravia's, if not London's, most prestigious addresses.

Bay had watched a documentary about some of London's most expensive properties, two of which had been on Eaton Square. They parked around the corner in a pay and display bay on a street called Elizabeth Street. Despite being in Zone One, it had such a village vibe with a pet shop, various coffee shops with pastel-coloured awnings and a pretty florist with the most gorgeous flower wall outside framing the window in reds, yellows, blues, pinks and white. There was a little elephant-shaped bush outside that was for sale. As Bay stopped to admire the window display, she reached out to touch a flower to see if it was real... but it wasn't.

'Some of the prettiest things in this world aren't as real as you're led to believe,' Mia sounded more like a prophet than her usual self-obsessed self and Bay again wondered if there was more to her than met the eye.

Bay bent down to look at the price of the elephant shaped bush, but after seeing its £125 price tag she stifled a gasp of horror and swiftly moved on before the shop assistant could come out and try to pressure her into making an unnecessary and overpriced topiary purchase.

They turned the corner to see the beautiful, private gated gardens of Eaton Square. The foliage seemed greener here and she could hear children playing on the grass, and sprinkler systems spraying away keeping the little oasis in the City centre in full bloom.

Perfectly-kept hedgerows and grand trees protected the gardens, giving an element of secrecy and privilege.

'Wow! I'd love to live on one of the garden squares,' Bay said, trailing her hand along the wrought iron fence that separated London's wealthiest inhabitants from the riff-raff on the pavements.

'No need, they open them once a year to the public for a weekend. It's a great day out,' Mia smiled.

Bay made a note to look up the Open Garden Squares Weekend on her phone. She simply must buy tickets and explore these private sections of paradise. They reached a padlocked gate and she got a proper look inside. There was a tennis court to the left and a lush green plot of grass to the right surrounded by benches. The two areas were separated by a beautiful bed of exotic-looking flowers, none of which Bay recognised by name apart from the one solitary sunflower in the middle, standing tall and exposing its face to the sun. It was a mini oasis in SW1.

They arrived outside Max and his dad's house and Mia took out a key. The property had a small canopy over the entrance door like a New York apartment block.

'So, which floor are they on?' asked Bay, looking up at the four-storey Victorian building and squinted in the sun as her eyes took in the top floor with a little Juliette balcony surrounded by its own wrought iron railings to match the garden square it looked over.

'All of them!' replied Mia, turning the key to the pastel green door, the colour of which matched a little

Nissan Figaro car parked outside and Bay noticed what a great Insta picture it would make.

Her image of the perfect picture was interrupted by a loud beeping from the house as Mia had set off the alarm system by inserting the wrong code. She quickly corrected her mistake and the bleeping stopped, returning peace to Belgravia once more.

Bay stepped inside and was completely taken aback, in a good way, by the interior. With the building's ancient-looking outside, she'd expected to find a dark but cosy English manor house inside with mahogany walls and green carpet! In fact, it was like something out of a Scandinavian interior design magazine. There were literally no walls between the entrance hall and the back of the building and she could see all the way through to the glistening white kitchen with island unit and out through the bi-folding glass doors to the manicured garden beyond.

Although the house was narrow it went back a long way. Probably the result of extension after extension, thought Bay, having driven past many houses undertaking building works on the Chelsea streets.

The floors were a light wood colour and all the walls were white apart from the one running the length of the right-hand side which was exposed brick. This housed a built-in TV which must have been about 50' and a matte black, rectangular fireplace in front of the dining area. Even the dining table was an impressive piece of architecture in its own right, a huge piece of natural marble, framed on one side with a stone bench covered with a wool mat, and on the other was four plastic see-through chairs. The large room also contained a grey velvet curved sofa and two mustard-coloured bucket seats, also in velvet with a brown wooden coffee table in the middle. On the coffee table sat a selection of property magazines and Bay recognised Max's dad's face on the top cover.

'Come on, I'll show you around,' Mia called, already heading down a set of stairs back in the hallway. The smell of chlorine greeted them as they proceeded down and Bay thought, no it couldn't possibly be, but yes, this place did indeed have an indoor swimming pool! Bay stood open-mouthed as they opened the door to reveal a square pool. It was small, but a pool none-the-less. There was a further set of bi-folding doors; these were tinted and led out to a small seating area and a spiral staircase back up to the main garden.

The rest of the house consisted of five bedrooms. The master took up the entire first floor with a huge ensuite containing his and her showers, a stand-alone bath tub looking out on to the garden and a walk-in wardrobe that could have been a room in its own right, containing a pouffe seat in the middle, again in velvet, of course.

They reached the fourth floor where the office was located, in the room with the Juliette balcony. There were two giant Mac computers sat on white desks and a large, industrial size photocopier in the corner. There were pop art style pictures of London landmarks on the walls in white frames which added a much-needed splash of colour.

Mia sat down and began clicking on one of the computers. She logged into her email, found the contract from Archie and clicked 'print'.

'Oh, bloody technology!' she muttered, as no sound seemed to be coming from the printing device. 'Ah!' she said in triumph as she pressed the 'on' button and the machine whirred into action. She clicked 'print' again but still nothing happened. 'For goodness sake!' She threw her arms down like a child who'd just been told they couldn't have the cuddly toy they so desperately wanted. 'Bay, can you turn that one on, while I see if I can fix this.'

Bay wiggled the mouse around on the other computer until the screen flashed up asking for a password or if you wanted to use face recognition. She clicked 'face recognition' for a laugh to see what it was all about and the screen shook disallowing her access. There was a sticky note with six numbers written on stuck on the wall above the computer. Bay typed them in, and the computer made a successful ping. Max's dad's logo 'Merrygold Holdings' was plastered across the screen.

The printer began to print. 'About bloody time!' Mia wiped the smallest of sweat droplets from her brow, like that was the hardest bit of work she'd done in months.

She picked up the first page. 'Better have a skim read,' she said. 'Oh no, this isn't my contract! What the...' Her voice dropped off and she wafted the paper in front of Bay's face for her to read.

It was a letter, a brief one that read:

Dear Richard

In a shark-infested, dog eat dog industry such as ours you really should be more careful about who you attempt to screw over.

Karma has a funny way of dealing with such issues, so I suggest you and your family keep a watch out a little more from now on.

It was signed MM.

Realising the seriousness of what she had just seen, Bay dropped the piece of paper in panic.

'Oh my God, it's a threat to Amy's dad!'

CHAPTER 11

'It's time to point the finger but
we don't have enough hands!'

After finally printing Mia's contract, the two girls drove speedily back to Olivia's, probably a little quicker than the legal speed limit allowed. Luckily, no cameras had flashed, at least Bay hoped they hadn't, as being in more trouble with the police is not what they needed. Bay was convinced they would be taken down, one speeding fine at a time.

They pulled up outside Olivia's and scurried in. Molly was watching repeats of *Friends* on the television and Olivia was on the floor still reading Vogue, one hand in a bowl of cheese puffs.

Mia and Bay showed them the letter.

'Bloody hell!' exclaimed Olivia, spitting bits of cheese puff everywhere.

'Surely you don't think Mr Michael Merrygold would push Amy off the balcony over some silly property feud, do you?' Molly read the letter again.

'Some silly property feud to you and me is actually millions of pounds to the developers, Mol,' Mia reminded the girls of the lucrative, if cut-throat, industry.

It was no secret that Michael Merrygold and Richard Braybury were both successful property people, but what had gone so wrong to warrant a threat like that was beyond Bay.

'Do you think I should take it with me and show it to the police?' Mia asked, looking at her watch. It was 3.30pm and she'd need to leave at 4pm for her interview... or was it going to be an interrogation?

'Absolutely not! If he did target Amy and push her off the balcony as some sort of sick revenge, think what he will do to you if he finds out you gave him up!' Olivia sat bolt upright from her relaxed position on the floor.

'Yeah, true, we don't know how dangerous he is, Mia. Maybe don't mention this to Max yet either,' Molly shared her concerns.

'Definitely don't show it to Max!' Olivia grabbed the note from Mia, rolled it up, put it into the pocket of her Juicy Couture tracksuit and sat back to rest against the sofa. 'I'll keep hold of it until we know what's actually going on,' she said, tapping her pocket. 'Now what could have gone so wrong between them?'

'I've got an idea!' Bay knew how to dig dirt on a subject, from her old newspaper job. She pulled Olivia's laptop out from under the sofa and typed in Michael Merrygold's name. The only things that came up were the website MerrygoldHoldings.co.uk and an article from three years ago about an old people's home he'd launched in Chiswick.

'Hmmm,' Bay murmured, momentarily stumped in her research. She then retyped Michael Merrygold and put Richard Braybury's name next to it. She hit 'search'.

'Bingo!' She pumped one fist in the air.

The girls gathered round on the floor. Bay had come across a website called Property Today and the title of the article read 'Multimillionaire Michael Merrygold's minor mistake maxes out mogul's monies'.

'It says that Michael Merrygold invested over £143 million on a disused Chelsea barracks site. After spending a further £100,000 on planning application after planning application, for them only to be rejected, he was forced to sell at auction to the highest bidder. Re-selling for £98 million, he made a loss of over £45 million. If that wasn't bad enough, a rival developer, Mr Richard Braybury, was the anonymous bidder and has just been granted planning using Michael's original blueprints but adding winter gardens instead of balconies to the description of the outside space and allocating 30% to retirees at reduced costs.' Bay paused.

'£45 million, that's a hell of a lot of clothes,' Olivia added.

'That's a hell of a lot of anything!' said Bay. 'But what does it all mean?'

'It means, basically, Richard Braybury had some insider info and used it to fuck over Mikey's plans. Not cool Richard, not cool!' explained Olivia.

'But to push someone's daughter off a balcony?' Molly glumly reminded everyone of the situation.

'Money makes you do stupid things, just look at Justin Bieber with that haircut!' Olivia pointed down at an article in Vogue, showing Justin Bieber with a bright platinum blond tuft of hair on his head. The article was comparing him to a cockatoo and they even had a little 'who wore it best' picture of the Bieber next to one of the funny looking parrots.

'I'd better get going, my car's outside,' Mia announced, after looking at her phone.

'All right. Good luck. We'll see you at the White Horse around seven, yeah?' Olivia waved.

'Right, let's plan this out,' Olivia said once Mia had shut the door.

'Plan what out?' Molly looked more confused than ever.

'This whole thing. Who did it?' Olivia said between gritted teeth, holding a pen whilst she reached for a sketch book on top of her kitchen cupboard. She brought it back to the floor and began drawing a brain-storm style diagram. 'Now let's write down everything we know, times, motives, suspects.'

Bay and Molly shouted out things they knew whilst Olivia squiggled on the paper.

'Time – pushing around 8pm,' said Molly.

'Michael Merrygold's threatening letter to Richard,' added Bay.

'Amy not getting the role,' Molly again.

'Archie and his oddness this morning,' wrote Olivia.

'Liv!' Molly looked hurt as her friend wrote down her boyfriend's name under 'suspects'.

'Did you not see the way he acted this morning, trying to get Mia to say that she was with him at the time Amy fell? Where was he that evening before he nearly flattened me with the door?' Olivia asked.

'He said he had to take care of something,' replied Molly quietly.

'Says it all, doesn't it?' Olivia was pushing boundaries.

'Mia!' said Bay suddenly, trying to move the conversation on from Archie.

'What about Mia?' snapped Molly.

'She was the last one to see Amy alive and then she disappeared at the event. Now the police want to talk to her.' Bay tried to explain her thinking.

'You're both mad!' Molly said in a high-pitched voice and jumped up. She made her way to the door. 'This is just another conspiracy theory you think you can play with. Don't you see that you're blaming my boyfriend and our best friend for something terrible we know they'd never do?' Molly could still be heard wailing as she went down the stairs even after she'd left the flat and slammed the door behind her.

'I do love a good conspiracy theory though, she's right!' giggled Olivia. 'Oh, don't worry, she'll come round after she's mulled it all over and we'll probably hear from her again this evening.'

Bay wasn't sure if she had made a mistake and added fuel to the fire by saying Mia's name. She had to admit she had got a bit carried away with the whole playing detective thing. Who were they kidding thinking they could actually solve the crime? She was about to press Olivia for her thoughts when her friend, seeming to read her mind, said, 'Don't worry about the Mia thing. I get that it looks suspicious, but I think that there's more to her story.'

Bay agreed but instead of saying anything else that might damage Mia's innocence, she nodded and added, 'Yeah, and likewise with Archie. I get it. He was acting suspiciously and he was the one who asked Mia to invite Amy in the first place.'

'No way, shut up, when?' asked Olivia busily adding notes to the board.

'At the Bluebird, he said it would be good for her reputation,' explained Bay.

'What a bizarre thing, well as much as Molly wants to deny it, this certainly puts him on the list.' Olivia drew a circle around Archie's name and Bay wondered how her first few days in London had gone from job hunting to crime solving in such a short space of time.

Suddenly both Bay and Olivia's phones pinged at the same time. Bay looked at Olivia and then they both turned their eyes to their phones. It was from Mia, 'Please could you come and get me, this is not good!'

CHAPTER 12

'Time will reveal what inter-rogation can't.'

Bay had been fighting the traffic as it crept closer to rush hour as well as the after school club pickup time and had to deal with Chelsea tractor mums in their G Wagons and Cayennes attempting to squeeze through gaps they thought were too narrow for their luxury SUVs although anyone else could have driven a bus through – or they would suddenly stop and drop off a child or two outside a double fronted house, holding up the entire road with complete disregard for the other road users. Not to mention turning left without any form of indication and almost mowing down cyclists left, right and centre.

The police station was a dark square block of concrete with a little blue sign on the front reading Metropolitan Police. Bay used to live about 100ft from a local police station in Watergate Bay and always felt safe knowing they were down the road. She even knew the Chief Constable, Roberto, on a first name basis. He'd walk round the streets in the evening and her father would offer him a shot of Disaronno to keep him going on a night shift.

But this was different. She parked outside the soulless grey structure and grimaced at how unfriendly it looked. She tried calling Mia but there was no answer. She began to wish she had forced Olivia to come with her, then she could have waited in the car and sent Olivia off to find Mia. Olivia for once actually had some work to do in the form of a video call to a client and didn't think that a police station would make the best backdrop for such a call and was most put out that she would be missing out on the big reveal of whatever Mia had found out at the station. They had agreed to meet at their usual spot in an hour.

Bay hurried up the steps and through the automatic glass doors. After glancing around the empty room she quickly manoeuvred herself over to a reception desk manned by an elderly grey-haired woman with glasses.

'Hi,' said Bay with a friendly smile.

'One moment, love,' replied the woman, squinting at the computer screen in front of her without even looking up.

After a further minute of no response, Bay tried again.

'I'm here to collect someone,' she said pressing call next to Mia's number again but still with no response.

'Take a seat,' the woman pointed towards some blue plastic chairs, again without making any kind of eye contact.

'Thanks,' replied Bay despondently, as she walked towards the chairs.

The double doors to the right of the reception desk flew open with a loud bang which made Bay jump. A blonde woman came bursting through the door, her ponytail swinging side to side as she lolloped along. Behind her was Mia who seemed to breathe a sigh of relief when she saw Bay and then a youngish man with a good head of brown hair and a tan to match Mia's sun kissed skin. They escorted Mia over to the reception desk where she appeared to sign something. The man smiled at Mia but the woman folded her arms and scowled at her. Bay took this as her cue to leave too and got up quickly, eager to get out of the building. She caught up with Mia in front of the glass doors and they rushed down the steps and back into Bay's car.

'That was not fun!' Mia sounded stern as she shook her body like a dog after a bath. 'I do not want to relive that again, in fact I think I'd rather just forget the whole ordeal!'

'Well you'll have to tell it at least once more, I know Olivia will be waiting with baited breath! I'm sure she'll already have a bottle on ice though so at least that will help with erasing all memory of the day!' Bay gave a little laugh at her own banter. 'So tell me what happened?'

Mia explained how she was led down a brick-lined corridor that was dark and unwelcoming and into a little side room. 'I had seen rooms like it on TV shows and knew what to expect.' She continued, 'Constable Harry Hirst was a really nice guy, he seemed to understand or maybe that was his way of getting all the information out of me but Detective Laura Winston had the worst resting bitch face I've ever seen, she looked as though she could get you to confess to anything!'

'Yeah she looked scary!' Bay added trying to sound supportive.

'I was aiming for cool, calm and collected but not confrontational, but she really knew how to push my buttons!' Mia then began to put on some kind of East End accent. Bay presumed she was impersonating Detective Laura Winston. 'You must be used to this type of interview in your business, what with your new film being announced as well. Except remember this isn't Heat magazine, darlin', this is real life, and someone is dead.'

'Wow she really went in for the kill!' Bay didn't like where the tone of the story was going. As she drove through the London streets, she wondered more and more what Mia had meant by her text, 'this is not good'.

'Yeah I realised why Archie had been prepping me. It was like an audition! Anyway, then I told the story, from the audition and the script mix-up, to the conversation on the rooftop balcony. I was 100% honest.' Mia paused and guiltily looked at Bay.

'What?' Bay took her eyes off the road for a second to look at Mia who had an expression on her face of a toddler that had just drawn all over the walls of a house.

'I did what Archie advised and said I had been with him between speaking with Amy and the realisation that she had fallen off the balcony.' Mia looked deflated.

Bay tried not to look disappointed. She knew lying was not the way forward in any situation but she could see how desperate Mia was and it sounded like the police weren't on her side. It wasn't looking good for Mia, Bay couldn't help but think back to earlier in the afternoon when even she herself had listed Mia as a suspect. 'Did they say anything?'

'Yes that's the big problem! When I said that about being with Archie, Laura had this sly little side grin. She then grabbed a TV remote, aimed it at the telly and told me to describe what I saw.'

'You're kidding, it was the CCTV?' Bay was once again pleased with her skills of piecing things together.

'Yes, exactly! The footage was from the main atrium looking out towards the doors before the balcony. We went out onto the balcony and then came Amy. This was followed by you, Olivia and Molly leaving. Then there were a couple of passers-by and waiters with canapés and then me leaving after the conversation.' Mia described the footage.

'Then what?' Bay was beginning to overheat with the anticipation of what Mia had seen next on the CCTV.

'Then they paused the tape and said, 'Tell us who this is, do you recognise this man?' They clicked 'play' again and Archie walks towards the balcony door, pulls it open and heads out.'

CHAPTER 13

'Is it really breaking and entering if you have a key?'

Olivia was already half way through a bottle of rosé when Bay and Mia arrived at the White Horse. She was sitting at the same table as always, which was still hanging onto the very last rays of the evening sun. It was becoming Bay's favourite part of the day, when all the girls would get together and discuss this and that over a bottle or two as they watched the sun set on another balmy London summer evening. Anyone watching them would think they were living the life, not that they had been dragged into the middle of a murder case.

'Hi.' Olivia kissed the girls quickly on both cheeks as she whizzed around like a tornado at the table.

Bay helped herself to the remnants of the rosé and poured a glass for herself and Mia.

'Hey!' Olivia, at first, sounded a little annoyed at the disappearance of her wine before she realised that meant another bottle was definitely needed. 'Shall I get another?' It was more of a statement than a question as she'd already disappeared across the terrace before either Bay or Mia had time to answer.

Mia let out a puff of air and tied her long brown hair up in a bun. She took another gulp of the wine as Olivia hurtled back from the bar, twisting the screw cap off the bottle of wine as she ran as fast as her Jimmy Choos would allow her. She topped up everyone's glasses with the pale, cool liquid, which was so cold that the glasses began dripping with condensation.

'OK, go!' Olivia said, picking up her own glass and leaning over the table to give Mia her full attention.

'OK,' began Mia. 'They asked me everything, what we'd discussed, what my conversation with Amy was about, whether there was any bad blood between us, if I'd seen anyone else talk to Amy and who else I'd spoken to that evening.'

Olivia nodded listening intently, knowing that there was more to come.

'Then there was a video,' Mia continued.

'The hotel CCTV?' Olivia butted in to clarify.

'Yes, you could see us go out to the balcony, then Amy comes in and joins us, then you guys leave and then I leave and then this guy comes in and they asked me if I recognised him.'

'Who was it?' Olivia was so excited that she nearly spilt her drink.

'Archie,' Mia whispered for effect.

'Archie?' Boomed Olivia 'What the fuck! He didn't tell us he'd talked to her. Not to mention him saying he'd be your alibi. Mia, he wanted you as *his* alibi. We need to tell Molly. But first, what did you tell the police?' Olivia was all over the place with this fresh bit of information.

'I told them it was Archie. They knew I'd already lied about being with him, so I had to tell them the truth and that he'd asked me to say that we'd been together.' Mia retold the story.

'It's not looking good for Archie.' Olivia shook her head with disappointment.

'So, shall we call Molly?' Bay added. She really wanted to clear the air with her new friend and warn her about what they had found out. She knew there was something suspicious going on with his behaviour that morning and Molly saying that he had been acting oddly.

Olivia dialled Molly's number from her favourites list. A picture of Olivia and Molly dressed as schoolgirls for Halloween flashed up on the screen.

'Cute,' joked Mia.

'Good times!' Olivia gave one of her winks.

'Liv,' said Molly's voice on the other end of the phone. 'Archie's been taken in for questioning. I'm so pleased you called. Look, I'm sorry for flipping out earlier but I don't understand what's happening.' Molly was talking fast in a panic.

'Mia's back from the police station. We're at the Sloaney, you'd better come here. I think you need to hear this,' Olivia said.

Molly was there within ten minutes.

Olivia had collected a fourth glass from the bar along with another bottle of wine, again zipping back to the table, not wanting to miss a millisecond of any gossip.

Mia repeated her police station saga to Molly. 'Sorry, Mol, but I had to tell the truth,' she finished.

'It's OK, I get it. But what was he doing talking to her? That's what I can't understand.' Molly looked puzzled.

Bay looked at Mia. She remembered that she hadn't shared the events they'd overheard at the Kensington Club on that first night out, how Amy was trying to get Archie to sign her to his books to represent her and how Archie had said 'you won't be around much longer'. Things were starting to add up.

'I think we need more answers,' Olivia said boldly, as she finished off the remainder of her glass, looked at the three empty wine bottles, and stood up.

Bay knew this was a sign that Olivia had hatched one of her plans. They looked expectantly at her for further instructions.

'We'll go to Archie's,' she said to three shocked and baffled faces. 'Well, he's not going to be there is he? He's banged up for all we know, and we can't sit around here playing guessing games all evening, can we?'

Molly was the first to compose herself and she nodded in agreement. 'I've got to know what he's been up to!' She got up ready to follow Olivia.

'But how will we get there? And when we do get there, what are we looking for?' Mia asked, looking somewhat reluctant to get involved in Olivia's plan. Bay didn't blame her; Olivia's plans were always a bit hit or miss. Back in

Cornwall, there had been a local bit of filming for some period drama and Olivia had suggested they go along to see if they could sneak in as extras. They had to be physically removed from the set as they had borrowed costumes reserved for Meryl Streep. This was in front of hundreds of onlookers, all with live videos broadcasting to the world and Bay had been mortified when they'd made the events page of Cornwall Life magazine. Although Olivia had pointed out that they got way more exposure than simply being extras, so that must have been where her PR career started.

'I don't know what we're looking for, what murderers hide maybe? Molly, you're into all that detective crap. You're always watching *Living Next Door to a Murderer* and *My Neighbour's a Serial Killer* on those true crime channels. Any tips? Or maybe that's where he got his ideas from! Hmmm?' Olivia cocked her head to the side waiting for Molly's reaction.

Too far, Liv. We don't know Archie is actually guilty, maybe we're looking for something to prove his innocence,' Bay said, feeling protective of Molly.

Molly gave Bay a smile filled with gratitude.

'Good point, newbie! To the car!' Olivia held out her arm like a sergeant leading their troops into battle.

'You can't expect me to drive, did you not see the three empty bottles?' Bay pointed to the table.

'Yes, but you've only had like two glasses, you're such a slow drinker. You'll be fine. The police in London have much more to worry about than drink driving, like murder!' Olivia reminded her.

This is just what Bay needed to complete her introduction to London; first a near miss with a traffic warden, a possible speeding fine and now heading towards a DUI, not to mention being at a party where a girl was thrown off a balcony. But she had only consumed two glasses max and right now they needed answers.

They picked up the Fiat from Olivia's, who ran in to change her shoes but came out in a black hoodie and New York Yankees cap, looking every bit the street thug.

'Really blending in there, Liv,' joked Mia as they got into the car.

'We are going to Brixton!' Olivia shot a glance back at Mia.

'Clapham,' corrected Molly.

'Close enough.' Olivia shrugged.

Archie, in fact, lived on the border of Clapham and Battersea in a lovely residential neighbourhood, home to many young families, hence the area was nicknamed 'Nappy Valley'.

'Don't park right outside!' whispered Olivia as Bay began to pull into a space. 'What, have you never done a stake out before?' She looked at the other girls.

'No!' all three replied in unison.

Olivia rolled her eyes. 'We'll park around the corner, there on the end so we can make a quick getaway.'

Bay daren't ask Olivia if she herself *had* in fact been on a stakeout before. It was probably just Olivia living her life like a movie, as she always does. Bay pulled up on the end of a row of cars and they hopped out. Led by Olivia, they tiptoed down the street to the door of

Archie's flat. The entrance was split into two, one door led to the upstairs flat and the other to Archie's on the ground floor. Molly, of course, had a spare key and she turned the lock and they all squeezed into the hallway. Molly switched on the light.

'No lights!' hissed Olivia. 'Use your phones. Spread out and search for anything. Remember to make this owl sound if you hear anything suspicious.' Olivia cupped her hands together and made a 'whoo' sound.

'Liv, no offence, but I don't think I've ever heard an owl in Clapham,' Mia chuckled.

'What do you suggest then? Anyway, people will think it's an owl before thinking it's four girls breaking and entering making twit twoo noises,' Olivia defended herself.

Bay nodded. She did make a fair point.

Bay and Mia stayed in the living area whilst Olivia and Molly took the bedroom. From what Bay could make out, the kitchen and lounge were open plan at the back of the flat with French doors, painted in white, leading out from the kitchen to a little paved walled garden covered in vines and climbing rose bushes. It was a very country-style home with a little green Aga in the kitchen and brown wooden skirting. It was cute with contemporary furnishings, such as the grey corner sofa which Bay recognised from Ikea. They had just got an Ikea in Devon, which had been the closest one to her in Cornwall, and it was the highlight of the year in the West Country.

Mia began pulling open kitchen cupboards and sifting through any bits of paper she could find. They were mainly instructions for the appliances and not any murderous plotting plans. Bay focused on the lounge, looking for a laptop. After her success at cracking the login at Max's house, she was feeling confident with her technology abilities. There was no such luck as she couldn't locate any kind of computer let alone attempt to browse its contents. She pulled at the drawer of the TV cabinet which sprang open, only revealing stacks of DVDs. She shut it again in disappointment.

Then, as Bay headed over to the kitchen to join Mia, they heard a key being turned in the front door.

CHAPTER 14

'A picture tells a thousand words,
but a video tells a million.'

B ay and Mia looked at each other in horror. Who was coming in? Was it someone who had followed them? Was it the police? Was it Archie? They didn't hang around to find out. Bay, thinking on her feet, grabbed Mia's hand and they elegantly sprang, like a couple of gazelles, barely touching the ground, over to the French doors. As they heard whoever had come in taking off their shoes in the hallway, Bay twisted the key that was already in the door and slowly pushed it open, using both hands to steady it. She and Mia slipped out before turning to look for Olivia and Molly.

They were still in the bedroom. Bay could see them on the other side of the living room, about to creep across it towards the kitchen and the French doors. Suddenly the light snapped on in the hallway. Bay waved her hands from side to side in rapid motions signalling to Olivia and Molly to go back and then Bay pointed towards the bedroom window and made a 'w' sign with her thumbs and forefingers. She was getting quite good at this spy thing, she thought, proudly, maybe she had missed her vocation and should join MI5.

Her thoughts were brought back to reality as Mia made the loudest 'Ca-Caw' sound.

'What the hell are you doing?' whispered Bay in panic, she was now really beginning to sweat.

'Making the bird noise,' Mia shrugged as she whispered back.

'An owl, not an eagle,' scowled Bay.

The intruder came into the light and into the living room. It was Archie. Mia and Bay looked at each other in panic. If he'd murdered Amy, think what he might do to four females snooping around his home looking for evidence that would put him in a prison cell for the rest of his life. Mia gently closed the door and the two of them disappeared to the side of the garden, just as Archie turned on the light in the open plan room, looking around, probably wondering where the hell the crazed pigeon sound was coming from outside his living room. Watching him from a side window into the kitchen, they could see him fumbling with a packet of cigarettes.

'Oh God, he's coming out for a smoke!' whispered Mia in fear as he crossed the kitchen towards the French doors.

'We've got to get the others.' Bay moved forward, treading carefully as she went so as not to disturb the ground beneath her. Luckily, Archie's building was semi-detached, so a little side corridor ran to the front. They reached the bay window of the bedroom at the front of the property to find Olivia half in and half out of the sash window.

'Help me!' She reached out to grab Bay with her free arm. Olivia squatted over the windowsill like she was riding a horse and her hoody was stuck on the latch at the top.

'I'm going to have to rip it,' whispered Bay.

'Good riddance. I don't know what I was thinking,' Olivia said, swatting at the hoody, but she couldn't quite reach.

There was a tearing sound as Bay and Mia tugged furiously at the seams and eventually Olivia was freed and fell a short way to the ground. The sash window came hurtling down with a bang, bringing the rest of the hoody with it.

'Molly!' The three girls who had escaped tried unsuccessfully to lift the sash window from the outside, but Olivia's bit of hoody material had got tangled around the latch. The light came on in the bedroom and Archie stood in the doorway looking at Molly and then to the girls outside the window.

Olivia gave a weak wave at Archie before Mia slapped her hand down. As they turned to run away, the front door opened and Archie yelled.

'Girls, come back here. We need to talk.'

Not wanting to leave Molly, the others reluctantly headed back towards the flat and went inside.

'Sit down,' he demanded, aiming his hand in the direction of the Ikea sofa where Molly sat, holding some papers.

The atmosphere quickly turned from threatening, with Bay thinking they were about to become his next victims and be chopped up into little pieces and stored in his freezer, to friendly as he said, 'Tea anyone?' and proceeded to put the kettle on as he grabbed a bag of Tetley from the cupboard.

Surely a killer wouldn't waste time or teabags for that matter, thought Bay, clenching her fists, waiting for the next thing to happen. Olivia was peering over her shoulder, trying to read the papers that Molly gripped. Bay also turned her attention to the papers but all she could make out were coloured graphs with arrows on.

Archie handed out a cup of tea to each of the girls before fetching his own and pulled up a chair from the dining set to sit in front of them all. He looked exhausted, his usually slicked-back hair was splaying out of his head in spikes all over the place, his blue shirt was untucked and even his jeans looked a mess. He cleared his throat.

'I'm not even going to ask what the hell you're all doing here but now that I've explained it to the police, I guess I'd better tell you.'

They all sat in silence. Bay guessed no one dared say anything, although she had loads of questions in her head.

'So, yes, I went to talk to Amy after you left her, Mia. I'd been watching from outside and once I knew you had cleared the air with her, I thought I'd better do the same. We chatted for a couple of minutes and everything seemed fine,' he explained.

'But why didn't you tell us you'd spoken to her?' Molly began the questioning. Bay felt proud of Molly, she wasn't shying away from the situation, and she certainly wasn't about to shed a tear like Bay was expecting.

'Because she saw what I was doing, and I couldn't let it get back to anyone. You see as she was babbling away trying to explain herself, I got a text from my mate Steve,' Archie continued his story amidst sips of tea.

'Not suspicious Steve! What were you doing that no-one could know about?' Molly demanded in a firmer voice than she usually used. Clearly as per her description of this Steve character, he had a reputation for being up to no good.

Archie sighed as he unravelled the truth. 'Steve works in stocks and shares and that kind of thing. He's been giving me the heads up on what he's calculated is rising and falling, in exchange for a fee.'

Bay looked at the graphs which were all numbers and calculations that she couldn't make out. It was like going back to algebra class at school with all the Xs and Ys and brackets and funny looking symbols.

'Isn't that illegal?' Mia said, looking up.

'Last time I checked, insider trading is illegal, Mia, yes, which is why I couldn't tell anyone and why, when I saw Amy looking at my phone, I made her promise not to say anything and thought it was best not to mention the conversation at all. I was trying to escape being caught out cheating the system and I didn't even think about being a suspect in this whole thing.' Archie wiped his brow with the back of his hand. 'I'm so sorry Mol, I know I've been a bit shady recently, it all started spiralling out of control!'

'So, what did you tell the police?' asked Molly, putting her teacup back on its saucer.

'The truth, of course. I'd rather be charged for what I did than people even thinking I was in any way involved in Amy's death.'

'So, did you make any money?' Trust Olivia to ask what everyone else was thinking.

'At first, but then Steve got some bad information and I lost it all, so when he told me to invest when I was on the balcony with Amy, I knew I had to do it. I was in so much debt. Mol, I lost £160,000.' Archie's voice was broken as he looked down at the floor whilst rubbing his temple.

'What did the police say?' Bay asked, getting back to the point.

'Luckily they could rule me out of the murder because in the minutes Amy was being pushed, I was placing shares and they can track the exact times the shares were placed. I've had to pay back every penny I've ever earned plus a fine and I've lost my trading licence. But I've got off lightly. Fuck, Steve's going to kill me!' Archie dropped his head in his hands.

'And I'm going to kill Steve!' Molly said bitterly through gritted teeth. 'Where are you going to get that money from?'

Archie looked at Mia. 'Why do you think I was trying to get you to sign the contract? You have read it right, the up-front agreement?'

Mia shook her head embarrassed. Archie rolled his eyes.

'You're lucky I'm here to do this shit for you, mind you I guess that's what you pay me for. As soon as you sign the contract, I negotiated an up-front fee for you which means 20% comes to me,' he said in a business voice.

'Sound great!' exclaimed Olivia 'But admitting your shady back door trading, doesn't solve this murder.' Olivia pressed her fingers to her lips as she gave the matter more thought.

'No, not yet it doesn't, but did they show you the rest of the video?' Archie asked.

'Yeah, up to the bit where you were about to walk in,' Mia answered.

'But what about after that?' he questioned.

'No, that was it.' Mia sat forward, intrigued.

'About three minutes after I go in, there's a mad exodus of people, probably all heading for the meeting room and in amongst all the movement the camera is pushed down to face the floor. So, all you can see after that is legs and feet!' Archie was trying to act it out with his hands.

'Then what?' chimed in Bay

'Then that's it, just legs and feet for the rest of the evening.' He shrugged.

They all sat back in their seats, deflated, as the only new evidence to hand consisted of a variety of shoes on a crummy CCTV system. It was back to the drawing board with the very real scenario of a murderer still at large and very much still a danger.

CHAPTER 15

'It's a dog-eat-dog world.'

Everyone seemed very much back in a sane state of affairs by the following morning. Olivia headed into her office at a reasonable time. Molly had stayed at Archie's. Mia was flitting around town running errands and Bay was left to her own devices in Olivia's Fulham flat.

It was the first time she'd really been alone since being in London and she found this quite refreshing. It was another glorious, sunny day and she decided to take a stroll along the Fulham Road and into the park with her notebook and pen to plan her emails to various job vacancies. Olivia had suggested a magazine, which Bay was due to have a call with at mid-day, but the truth was Bay just didn't know where to go with her career. She'd done some reporting for a local paper back home, but did that count for much in the professional London journalism scene?

She hurried through her granola and yoghurt breakfast, sitting at the little two-seater glass dining table positioned in front of the window and looking out on to the residential Fulham Street below. The sun shone through the glass, beckoning her to join it outside. She couldn't wait to get out and explore. So, after washing up her breakfast things, she scooped up her handbag, popped her phone, notebook and pen inside, and headed out.

The heat hit her body as soon as she stepped onto the pavement. It was a different heat from the air back home, which was always that bit fresher due to the sea breeze. This heat in London was more claustrophobic and muggier. After wondering if she was, in fact, over-dressed for the temperature and should change, she decided against it and set off along the tree-lined street.

The wisterias on the houses were in full bloom and their scented purple heads hung over many of the door-ways and windows of Mimosa Street, and Bay, enjoying the spectacle, soon reached the main Fulham Road. She glanced at her watch, it was still only 9.30am and the street was buzzing with people and traffic.

She saw a sign pointing left towards Bishops Park and she continued to stroll along, doing some window shopping as she went. She passed a pretty pink-painted boutique selling clothing, accessories and gifts that had the most gorgeous orange scarf and cutest circular straw bag with matching boater hat in the window. No wonder Londoners are so well dressed when they had stores like this on every corner, she thought. Even the charity stores had Burberry trench coats and second-hand Stella McCartney bags in the windows, she discovered, as she passed two such examples only two doors away from each other.

These shops were interspersed with a healthy offering of eateries too. There were cake shops, a cute Italian offering take away pasta dishes for five pounds, a plush looking steak house and wine rooms, which Bay wondered if Olivia had discovered and if not, why not? It was the type of place Olivia should have shares in as it had 'Olivia' written all over it! Bay made a mental note to tell her friend about it later.

Finally, she reached a roundabout. On the other side sat an old-fashioned ice-cream stand containing the most delicious looking ice-cream; the pinks, greens and yellows of the thick Italian gelatos were hypnotising, and Bay wondered if 10am was too early to indulge.

She crossed at the zebra crossing and went into the park and even though it was a weekday, there were still a good number of people milling about. A group of young ladies were at an outdoor fitness class, taking it in turns to do laps of the park, Pilates on mats and weight-lifting. They were all sporting regulatory *Sweaty Betty* attire with swinging ponytails and reusable water flasks. There were joggers speeding along the Thames Path, a couple of lone dog walkers and a youngish looking guy with floppy mousy hair, a khaki tee-shirt and cream shorts with a pack of eight dogs.

The dogs varied in size and breed and included a muzzled German shepherd, a pug, a little ball of fluff that resembled a baby fox, a miniature black and tan dachshund, a shaggy mongrel, two white Maltese and a chocolate Labrador. He looked as though he had his hands full as the group of canines literally ran circles around him getting their leads in a tangle. As he attempted to untangle the mess, one of the little Malteses escaped and began legging it across the field, trailing its lead and looking like one of those wind up cars you pull back and it flies off when released.

'Luna!' called the guy, attempting to assemble the other dogs in hot pursuit of little Luna who was now heading straight for Bay with its little mop haircut bobbing as it ran.

'Hello, Luna,' called Bay in her best dog voice. 'Who's a pretty girl then? Come here, look what's this?' Bay bent down and held out her hand pretending there was something in it. To her joy Luna ran up to her and began licking her hand, her arm and soon her face. 'No, no Luna, too far, that's enough!' she laughed, pushing the excitable pooch off her lap and grabbing its lead.

The guy eventually reached her, panting like the ninth member of the pack.

'Thanks so much,' he puffed. 'Mrs Maynard would have been so mad if I'd lost one of the twins!' He flopped down beside Bay on the ground, picked up Luna and patted her.

'How do you look after so many dogs?' Bay questioned, staring at the man. He was actually older than he had first seemed from a distance and looked as if he had just run a marathon.

'They aren't all mine,' he laughed. 'Just Mungo here belongs to me. I'm a dog walker, so the others I just walk for my clients,' he explained. He then proceeded to name them all. Along with his own shaggy mongrel, Mungo, there were Luna and Larry the twin Maltese, Crumpet the dachshund, Barney the Pomeranian fluff ball, George the pug, Batman the Labrador (Bay couldn't help but start giggling at this point) and Mr Fudge, he finished, patting the muzzled German shepherd.

Bay couldn't stifle her giggles any longer and burst out laughing, loudly.

'I know,' said the guy. 'Quite the collection of bizarre dog names.'

'Mr Fudge!' Bay began laughing again and wiped a tear from under her eyes.

'Quite the handful. My assistant quit on me this morning, said she's off to Greece to chase the sun for the summer.' He wiped the sweat from his forehead back into his hair and Bay couldn't quite decide if the action was absolutely disgusting or quite sexy!

'I'm Ollie, by the way.' He outstretched a hand towards Bay.

'Bay,' she replied, taking his hand to shake.

'Unusual name.' And Bay then explained it like she did every time she met someone new who made the same comment.

She then went on to tell him that this was her first free day in London and how she'd really just arrived. She stopped short from telling him the bit about the murder though, better not to share any baggage with any strangers just yet!

'Cool. Don't suppose you're looking for a job and like dogs?' he asked, ruffling the top of Mr Fudge's head, who had begun drooling through his muzzle.

'Yes to both, funnily enough, but I'm a journalist and I've actually got an interview in an hour,' she said.

'Cool,' he said again. 'Well, if you change your mind.' He flicked her a dirty-looking business card and got up. 'Good luck in London, Bay, nice to meet you.' He waved as he was pulled away by his crèche of canines.

'Bye,' Bay waved back and got up, then continued her walk through the park. She headed towards the glistening river, and then walked through a water garden, over a little bridge, passed the children's sand pit and play-park where she found a little cafe. She ordered an orange juice and a chocolate chip muffin, paid and took them outside to sit in the sun. There were a couple of well-dressed mothers bouncing their toddlers on their knees and sipping tea, so Bay chose a table in the corner where she sat down, pulled out her notebook and pen and began to make notes to prepare for her interview.

At exactly 12 midday, her phone rang. It was Sally from the magazine that Olivia had set her up with for an interview. Sally's voice was friendly but very much to the point; she was clearly a busy woman.

The magazine was called All Over London and they had a selection of local versions too, including All Over Fulham, Wimbledon, Chiswick, Chelsea and Notting Hill. The role was for a freelance journalist and she'd be required to produce three articles a week for £150 an article. Attending events, press calls and visits to interviewees would be in her own time and considering she didn't have another option, besides dog walking with Ollie, she accepted the offer. At least she would have some kind of an income and it would be in the journalism field.

Her first piece was to be for the Chelsea edition. It was about the Chelsea Flower Show, which was coming up, and she was to go and have a sneak peek behind the scenes that evening.

Before Sally finished the conversation, promising to follow up with an email of the details for that evening, she had a further request which was like a bombshell to Bay.

'Now, I know you're running in Olivia's circles and you and I and the rest of London have one hot topic on our lips at the moment, the Mayfair Murder.' Sally dramatically described it in such a journalistic way. By adding an alliteration and an over-the-top narrative you had yourself a headline. She continued, 'For our main All Over London edition next month, we're all putting our heads together to do a double-page spread on the deceased and the story surrounding her death. So, search your brain for anything useful, any insider knowledge and word on the street would be much appreciated,' she sang, a little too joyfully for Bay's liking. 'We even have a healthy bonus structure in place for this story, so every nugget of information is money in the bank,' Sally finished as if she was making the most normal, if somewhat mercenary, deal.

'OK,' Bay replied, trying to sound enthusiastic about what she'd been asked to do before ending the call. She knew she'd been given a great deal, having just moved to the city and landing a job in an industry that was notoriously difficult to get into and not particularly well paid, but she was also aware that Sally knew Bay was in a weak and vulnerable situation with no job. Was Sally, in fact, just using her to get a scoop on an event that she knew Bay had attended and would have first-hand knowledge of now and going forward? An 'access all areas' pass into the crazy world she'd seemed to have got herself in the middle of?

A ripple of regret began to wash over her that soon turned into a tsunami of doubt, dread and panic. She knew she had done nothing wrong in accepting the job, but had she joined, by default, the big, bad city of scandal, lies, gossip, betraying friends and ultimately murder, which was more in line with an episode of *Gossip Girl*?

But whatever happened next, Bay knew she needed answers. She couldn't let the murder of a supposedly innocent girl go without doing her utmost to make sense of it and bring the perpetrator to justice. She made up her mind - that's just what she would throw her heart and soul into, starting this very evening.

CHAPTER 16

'Accidents happen?'

The four girls had agreed to meet like they had done every day, around 5pm at the White Horse. Coincidently, both Olivia and Mia were also attending the event that evening and Archie gave his ticket to Molly so they could all go together. Bay had spent the afternoon back at Olivia's prepping for the evening ahead. She had made a list of people who were going and who she wanted to chat to, including the girls from the Kate Spade shop who were taking part in #ChelseaInBloom where the local stores on the King's Road decorate their shop fronts in flowers in a competition for the best display. Kate Spade had won last year with a giant six-foot flamingo and she wanted to know what they had planned to top it this year.

She also wanted to speak to the Chelsea Pensioners, who lived just behind the site of the flower show. They were war veterans who now permanently resided in the Chelsea Hospital and wore the rosiest red coats and could often be spotted strolling the streets of Chelsea in their regal outfits. They attended the event every year en masse ever since it started, and she wanted to know how things had changed.

Also on the guest list for tonight was Michael Merrygold, so she could put her plan of investigating who murdered Amy into action. She was planning to interview Michael as well, although she knew it wouldn't make the magazine, at least she had an 'in' to talk to him.

'Cheers,' called Mia, raising a glass of freshly-poured rosé into the air to be clinked with everyone else.

Bay was really beginning to enjoy the routine they had in the mild spring evenings that would soon turn to summer. It would start to stay lighter later and their favourite little table at the White Horse would be clinging to the warmth of the last rays of sun for at least an hour longer. Bay sipped on the dry rosé. She'd always thought of herself as a sweet rosé kind of girl, but nothing could beat the crisp freshness of this ice-cold, pale-pink liquid they knocked back so quickly each day. The bar staff pretty much had it waiting for them before they even arrived.

'Oh, and congrats on the new job, Bay!' Mia said, raising her glass again.

'Yes, well done!' Molly lifted hers too.

'Thanks to yours truly.' Olivia patted herself on the back.

Although Olivia hadn't arranged the outfits for the evening's extravaganza, they had all gone for a similar theme – floral, of course. Bay, inspired by the fashionista mums she'd seen in the park, was wearing a blue floral maxi skirt with a white cropped tee shirt and a necklace from the little pink boutique shop she'd treated herself to as a personal reward for securing her first London job. It was a cobalt blue and white zigzag Aztec print set in replica silver, and it reminded her of something Grecian, maybe due to the colours. It led her train of thought back to Ollie, the dog walker from earlier, who had lost his only other staff member to a sunny Greek Island. She wondered if she'd made the right decision and if she would have been happier and more at peace as a fellow dog walker, maybe they could have set up a bigger company together. She allowed her brain to create this otherworld fantasy. She then remembered London was not the place to come to be happier and more at peace and the magazine role would allow her to do what she loved, surrounded by the people she had come to love. And not because they'd invited her as a tag-along but because, thanks to her new job, she was legitimately an invitation holder.

Max arrived to join the girls at the table, as his dad was a sponsor of the Chelsea Flower Show. He was, of course, invited and had offered to drive the girls there. Bay's professional journalist skills kicked in and she waved to him, pulled him up a seat between her and Mia, kissed him on both cheeks as the socialites did here and asked if he'd like a drink. He did not, but Bay was trying to use her charm and kindness to entice him into giving her an insight into his dad.

Now that Archie was clear of murder, there was little evidence to prove if it was, in fact, a murder or not apart from the CCTV of feet passing in the evening. That left the current main suspect as Michael Merrygold, with the threatening letter they'd found to Amy's dad. This was a huge clue that only the four girls knew about, even above the police.

Six pm was drawing near and they'd been asked to arrive promptly. Mia had to do a test run for a speech she was giving, so, although being fashionably late was preferred at these social occasions, tonight they'd better make the effort to at least be there within half an hour of the requested time.

They hopped into Max's black Mercedes G Wagon. It was pretty cool as far as cars go and probably the most expensive one Bay had ever sat in, other than the time she had gone to a Cornish Country Fair and had her picture taken in Chitty Chitty Bang Bang.

The dashboard of the G Wagon was like something from a spaceship; blue lights shone on the electric screens and little dials turned to tell you the direction you were heading in, how fast you were going and the average mile per gallon. The radio connected straight to his phone via Bluetooth and began playing Akon, a pop/rap artist from the 2000s.

'Er, no.' Olivia, who had called shotgun and jumped in the front as she always did, pressed 'sync' and connected her own phone to the system. She began playing Rhianna and the car became a karaoke box on the ten-minute drive along Cheyne Walk and Chelsea

Embankment to the flower show. The river sparkled in the evening sunlight and the bridges over the Thames looked so pretty... apart from the rows of backed-up traffic trying to cross from the north to the south.

They pulled into a little residential street just before the entrance to the show and Max, surprisingly, found a space large enough to accommodate his spectacular vehicle that was the size of a small tank. They jumped out and onto the pavement, another traditional London street with old stucco-fronted villas painted in pretty colours with the most beautifully kept front gardens that were full to the brim with miniature trees and colourful flora.

If you live next to the Chelsea Flower Show you'd better make an effort, thought Bay, smiling at the beautiful works of art.

Bay walked through the entrance like she was on a catwalk, oozing confidence and an air of importance. Mia waved goodbye as she was bundled off towards the stage. Bay excused herself, too, as she wanted to explore solo for a while and get her interviews done. They had agreed to meet in an hour for Mia's speech.

Bay walked through the area, which was the size of three football pitches. It was like an exhibition but just for gardening. There were plants you could buy, heavy duty equipment like mowers and chainsaws as well as smaller goods like trowels and pretty aprons. There were stalls full of seeds, fake grass in various materials and garden furniture galore. Not to mention, a whole area dedicated to actual garden designs. Each gardener in the competition had their own square section with a white picket fence, and had created the most wonderful displays, from wildlife to buildings to mini cities, each angle cut perfectly into whatever flower or tree was being used to form the shapes. The whole place smelled like freshly cut grass, one of Bay's favourite smells. Back home everyone used to get the lawnmower out as soon as a bit of spring sunshine appeared. The bees were certainly loving the floral displays; it was like one of them had reported back to the hive and informed the others of the best pollen around and they had descended en masse to have a look. Every bush was humming away with the little guys. Bay snapped away at a large bumblebee on a lavender bush, on her smart-phone, as she'd promised to get some pictures.

She then headed towards the green room for her interview with the girls from Kate Spade. On her way she bumped into Olivia tucking into a glass of Prosecco and a plate full to the brim of little canapés again.

'If ever I lose you Liv,' Bay laughed, 'I'll head to the closest waiter with a tray of canapés!'

'I haven't paid for an evening meal in the last two years, so the jokes on you,' quipped Olivia, gobbling up an entire mini biscuit covered in cream cheese and a tomato in one go.

Bay finished her interview with the two girls from Kate Spade. They were lovely and she got some great hints about their display this year; it was going to focus around their own brand and feature coloured bushes shaped like popular accessories such as bags, hats, sunglasses and a British classic, the umbrella! Although Bay was rusty, she felt really pleased with how her first interview had gone. She even managed to woo them with a titbit about box plants she had researched before the event, and in return they had given her a discount code to use in the store.

Now for something less fun, but more important. Bay scanned the room for Michael Merrygold, before she spotted him in front of a mirror checking his hair. She recognised his tanned skin and head of hair from the stage at the Mayfair Hotel the other day.

'Michael, hi, Bay here from All About London, just a couple of questions about "the business."' She reached out a hand which he shook firmly, every inch the businessman.

'Yes, sure, absolutely.' He escorted her to a little table. 'What would you like to know?' he asked, giving a friendly smile.

Bay began by playing it safe, asking him about the sponsorship and why he felt it was important for him to be part of the show and what he liked about Chelsea, the property market and his plans for new projects - that kind of thing.

After five minutes of warming him up, she went in for the kill.

'You and Richard Braybury have a volatile relationship, but how do you intend getting revenge on him for the Chelsea Barracks deal?'

He looked her up and down as his smile narrowed to a thin horizontal line. He cleared his throat. 'Yes, the

Chelsea Barracks were an unfortunate incident, it's a shame Richard needed to go behind my back. As for revenge, I believe that everything happens for a reason and the Barracks were a blessing in disguise, an opportunity for Merrygold Holdings to unearth a better deal and better establishment for the local community.'

Bay nearly gagged at the perfect PR rehearsed spiel Michael waffled to her. He was very good and very well prepared. She tried again. 'Yes, and so sad about his daughter, Amy. You were there that night, weren't you?'

'I was indeed. Such a tragedy at such a joyous evening of celebration. My thoughts are with Richard and his family.' He smiled the successful smile of a sly entrepreneur. 'Right, I'd better get going, another day, another speech for our close-knit community,' he recited, as he shook Bay's hand once more and walked hastily towards the stage.

Bay sighed. That had not gone as she had hoped. She thought she went in there like Vera on ITV, not like Sean Penn in *Hot Fuzz*. He fed her so much of what she was sure was bullshit. Talking about the close-knit community of Chelsea like it was some Cotswold village where Bob in the bakery would deliver Susan's freshly made bread to her doorstep every day! From what she had seen of Chelsea, it was a playground for the rich and famous where there was a new money versus old money divide and everyone was competing for the biggest house, the deepest basement conversion and the fastest sports car.

She looked at her watch, gathered her things and headed towards the small-scale stage. There were little red tables set up in front of it. There was a red London bus branded with Pimm's and a matching red phone box next to it, in front of which was a flurry of influencers taking it in turns to pose. Coming out of the door, kicking their legs and pretending to be on the phone itself, all vying for the 'money shot' that would have the 'likes' rolling in in their thousands.

Bay spotted Olivia and Molly in the queue at the Pimm's bus. They were at the front and had been served two jugs of Pimm's with four red cups like the kind you get at American house parties.

'Hey girls,' Bay waved her hands in the air trying to get their attention. She succeeded and they trotted over, being very careful not to spill any drink on the way. They sat at one of the tables in the middle, ready to watch Mia's speech.

The stage itself was smaller than expected for an event of this size. It had a speaker system at each end and one line of speakers in the middle, along with a row of lights. The lights came on with a flash and then turned down to highlight the stage. Michael Merrygold walked out to a round of applause, taking an unnecessary little bow before giving a speech once more about Chelsea and its community. It was identical to his delivery to her questions earlier. He dedicated the event tonight to, 'Amy, who I knew through my dear friend, Richard, her father, and she had loved attending the event with him every year.'

Olivia scoffed, 'I don't know which PR has written this for him, but what a load of crap!'

Michael then turned around and scurried off the stage like a little rodent back to its hole, just as he had done at the Mayfair Hotel. Mia walked out on stage and waved to a few claps. Although she was quite well known online to the majority of 15-30 year olds, maybe gardening geeks and people over 50 hadn't much of a clue. Looking a little disheartened, Mia carried on. She was like a beauty queen on the stage; she carried herself well and her posture was straighter than a ruler. She spoke about how beautiful the displays were, and the weather and other lowbrow niceties.

Suddenly, in the middle of her describing her favourite kind of flower (the sunflower), the ladder holding the lights and speakers at the top of the stage fell down. Bits of speaker and lights were strewn across the stage, creating a cloud of dust. There was no sign of Mia.

CHAPTER 17

'Keep calm and party on.'

S ecurity flooded in from every angle and everyone rushed to the stage. Mia had been knocked forward onto the grass at the front of the stage and half-caught by one of the Chelsea Pensioners. She was unscathed and even posed for a picture, kissing her saviour on the cheek for a newspaper. Bay had been on edge ever since the murder. She didn't know how much more shock she could take; her emotions were like a rollercoaster being jerked and thrown about all over the place. From the sheer terror and crash of the lights falling down on the stage and Mia not being visible, to the next minute Mia hugging a Chelsea Pensioner for a photo op, which was the cutest thing ever.

'Geez, are you OK?' Molly asked, looking at her friend, checking for signs of injury.

'Bloody lucky I'll say. Health and safety will have a field day.' Olivia looked around for who was in charge.

A young woman with a clipboard was running towards them.

'Let me handle this.' Olivia took control, turning to face the woman.

'I'm so awfully sorry, are you OK? I've got the medic here to check you over. I'm so sorry again, we'll have a word with the Production Team,' sympathised the woman.

'No, no I'm fine, really,' Mia responded politely.

'Have a *word* with the Production Team. I think you should fire their arses. She could have been killed!' Olivia bleated. 'Who is the Production Team anyway? I'd like a word with them myself!' she finished, sharply.

'I can't tell you I'm afraid. GDPR,' explained the woman.

Olivia's eyes widened in disapproval. 'Fucking GDPR, it's taking the piss nowadays,' she growled, knowing it was a way to avoid any kind of PR nightmare or releasing any form of information. Bay disliked the whole GDPR thing too. The last time she had gone to her beauty salon to get her upper lip waxed with her normal therapist, Jade, she was told by the receptionist that Jade was on holiday. In passing conversation when Bay had asked 'where?' the receptionist responded by saying that she couldn't tell her because of GDPR. Like she was going to stalk Jade down to her country of vacation for a lip wax!

'We actually have a table booked for four people for dinner tonight, if you'd like the reservation it's on us,' smiled the woman, clearly trying to bribe them into not publicising the accident.

'No, it's OK,' began Mia. Olivia touched Mia's arm lightly to stop her talking.

'Where?' asked Olivia, bluntly.

'The Tropical Beach Club,' replied the woman.

'We'll take it!' Olivia was now towering over the woman using all her force to make sure they got that table.

'Liv?' Molly questioned her friend.

'What? That place is booked up for *months*. I've been on the waiting list since January. Me, the PR queen hasn't even had the luxury of going yet!' Olivia raised her hands with clenched fists in the air and did a silent 'yay'.

They were provided with a luxurious taxi to take them to the Tropical Beach Club, just a few minutes away, situated between South Kensington and Knightsbridge. Everyone was quiet in the cab ride there. Olivia had spent most of the time fixing her lipstick, meanwhile Bay was mulling over the seriousness of what could have happened to Mia on the stage.

They pulled up on the Old Brompton Road next to a restaurant called Aubaine and looked around for the entrance, but it was not obvious. They walked a little further along where they saw a couple of other people queuing.

'Are you going to the Tropical Beach Club?' Bay asked them. The girls in the queue nodded and went back to snapping more pictures for their social media stories.

Bay loved these inconspicuous hiding spots for the sought-after restaurants. It's like if you didn't have the savvy insider knowledge, you were meant to walk on by, oblivious to the buzz of twenty-somethings having the best night of their lives just metres behind the city walls. Their IDs were checked by a bouncer on the door and they were ushered inside like they were entering one of the world's best kept secrets. Just taking the first step into this place, Bay knew it was going to be incredible.

They first had to walk through a light tunnel which had changing rainbow lights flickering above them, on the floor and both walls. It was kind of making her dizzy but was absolutely stunning. At the end of the rainbow there was a woman in a bright, fuchsia-pink suit. She welcomed the girls with a Hawaiian lei each that she popped over their heads to hang around their necks. She then disappeared behind a black door and came back with an orange and red cocktail which they called 'virgin on the beach'. Bay took a sip from the bird-shaped glass. It was so sweet but so good with hints of orange and passion fruit. The colours mixed together to form a sunset-hued blend. The lady then opened another blacked-out door to reveal the restaurant itself.

It was like something out of a movie. There was the biggest neon sign that Bay had ever seen hanging from the back of the room, lighting up the restaurant name in pink. The restaurant was in a warehouse-style building with large tinted windows at ceiling height and at the sides. There was a mezzanine level in front of the neon sign where a DJ stood behind her decks, jamming away. The outside perimeters of the restaurant were covered in sand and there were large planted palm trees hanging over the tables below. Beside the DJ there was a trio of dancing girls who looked like they belonged on Kylie's *Showgirl* tour or at the Rio carnival. They were wearing bodysuits in pink, green and blue, which were covered in feathers with huge feather tails looped around behind them, attached to their toned behinds. They had glittery headpieces covering their foreheads, sprouting three large coloured feathers matching with their outfit colour schemes.

Bay, Olivia, Mia and Molly were led through the wicker and glass topped tables and matching fan-backed chairs, waitresses weaving through them wearing coconut bikinis and jewelled stickers on their faces like they were at an Ibiza beach party. The atmosphere was pretty much the same, minus the 30-degree heat. Their table was at the centre back and was set on its own little island with a bridge to it, one of three group tables sectioned off from the main restaurant by a pool of turquoise water. Bay wondered how many tipsy people had stumbled or fallen into it on a messy night out, but looking around she didn't spot anyone who appeared to have over-indulged on the juice. Bay guessed you may have to be a certain calibre of person to come here, or exceptionally well off.

She opened the menu at the table. Her jaw must have dropped open as Olivia looked at her and said, 'Don't worry, dinner's on them for nearly killing off Mia. So, what are you thinking then, whole lobster with truffle linguine?'

Bay scanned the menu for the lobster dish, it was £498, and she wondered why it was not just a round £500 guessing it must make it look slightly cheaper to begin with a four! As it turned out, they did not order the lobster but a selection of smaller dishes to share:

barbecued pork chops in a Jack Daniels sticky sauce, blackened cod in a sweet and sour vegetable mix, DIY duck and hoisin pancakes and some spicy chicken balls with a blue cheese dip.

As they were nibbling away, Mia's phone rang. It was Archie. She answered whilst balancing the phone to her ear with her chin. She licked the sticky sauce from her fingers and gave some 'uh huh' and 'yeah' responses to Archie. She put the phone down again.

'That was Archie saying he had heard from Carl Baker what had happened and asking was I OK.'

'Oh, I didn't realise Carl was there,' said Molly, taking a bite of another chicken ball.

'Nor did I, but apparently he's going to call me shortly,' replied Mia, tucking back into the dinner. She put her knife and fork back down and said, 'Girls, I was thinking and don't say I'm being dramatic, but don't you reckon it's a bit weird what happened tonight? I've been a bit on edge since the Amy thing and well, quite frankly, it's spooked me a bit.'

'What do you mean, like you don't think it was an accident?' Olivia said, half sarcastically through a mouthful of pork chop.

'I don't know. I mean, nothing like this has ever happened and I've been on stages most days of my life for the past two years.' Mia did look serious about her thoughts.

'Yes, but it only takes one dodgy member of the production team to forget a screw or something and boom. Accidents do happen, you know.' Olivia remained neutral despite Mia's accusations.

'Dodgy production team indeed. I did see a guy pulling ropes and things backstage just before I went on, but I didn't get a good glimpse of him,' Mia revealed.

'Nonsense. Why would you be targeted by a random stage-hand? Life isn't always about you, Mia.' Olivia took a sly dig at her friend, who responded by putting two fingers up.

'She could be right though, Liv. What if someone targeted Mia because she knows too much about the Amy thing? Remember the note on Michael's computer? What if he found out you had been there and now he's going to get you?' Molly had clearly been thinking the same as Mia and created this scenario in her head.

'Mmm, possible, but he's doing a shit job of getting rid of you. Taking his time, isn't he?' Olivia half-giggled whilst sipping another bit of her cocktail.

The more Bay thought about the situation, the more she thought Mia and Molly might be on to something. She began to panic. 'What if he saw us on one of the computer cameras or any other camera in the room?' she asked, looking at Mia for support.

'This isn't *James Bond*, people don't have spyware hidden in bookshelves in their homes.' Olivia was laughing.

'Yes they do, Liv, I've seen it in Selfridges, ties with cameras in and glasses and pens with voice recorders,' Molly described.

'Yeah and I tried to use the face recognition to get into the computer. What if he saw that?' Bay froze, realising the danger she could now also be in.

Olivia sat a little more upright in her chair as if she was coming around to their suggestions before reclining again making a 'hmph' sound, followed by, 'Ha, this is some *Goosebumps* shit, you're all freaking each other out!' Olivia became defensive when she was afraid to admit defeat and if she was feeling that something was amiss it wasn't boding well for any of them.

As they were all fretting about the situation, Mia's phone rang.

'It's Carl,' she said, answering. 'Hi Carl, how are you?' she asked coolly. 'Yeah I know, lucky escape.' She brushed off the evening's events lightly. 'Oh, um, I don't know... No way, are you serious? That would be amazing.' She grinned the largest grin and eyed up all the girls. 'Wow, well, if you're sure, I know they'd love to.' She clenched her fist and excitedly pumped her arm up and down.

'What, what is it?' Olivia half-screeched, half-whispered, barely able to contain her excitement for whatever was being discussed on the phone.

'OK, yes, pop me an email with the details and I'll confirm about the girls shortly. Thanks again, Carl, can't wait.' Mia ended the call. She turned to the girls. 'Oh my God,' she squeaked, almost bouncing off her seat.

'What?' Olivia had moved her seat so close to Mia's she was practically sat on her lap. It was as though she thought the closer she was, the quicker whatever

Mia was about to reveal would hit her ears before anyone else.

'Who wants to go to Dubai?' Mia was now completely out of her chair and stood up, holding her drink in the air.

'Meee!' Olivia shot like a rocket out of her seat with such force that some of her cocktail sloshed from her glass onto the floor.

'For real?' Molly was now standing in agreement too.

They all looked at Bay who clearly had a much more sensible head on her shoulders than the three other girls, who had already committed to taking a holiday at such short notice paid for by a man they didn't really know.

'Oh, Bay, things like this happen all the time. If it's not a free holiday, it's a free dinner.' Olivia read Bay's mind as she wafted her hand over the remains of the free meal they had devoured. 'You can write from there and I really think this is what we all need, to escape, particularly with a murderer on the loose. We'll be safe in Dubai. No one's going to try and pop anyone off there. I mean, they'll cut your hand off for not tipping your taxi driver!'

Bay looked at the girls, smiled and stood up to join the toast. Maybe this was what she needed, to live a little and Olivia had a fair point. Not much could get out of hand in Dubai.

CHAPTER 18

'Catch flights not feelings.'

The Dubai trip was just a day away. The girls had provided their passport details (via Mia) to Carl and they were booked on an Emirates flight from Heathrow to Dubai at 8pm Sunday, due to arrive bright and early in the morning with the eight-hour flight and time difference.

Bay had never been to Dubai, but she knew people who had. The general consensus was that it was like Marmite; she was either going to love it or hate it. Apparently, it was just like London with the same chains of fancy restaurants, such as STK, and other brands popular with the cool kids like Nikki Beach, Buddha Bar and China Whites. Although the weather was guaranteed sun all year, it was a city built in the desert, completely manmade from the millions of Sheiks and other high net worth individuals. It wasn't a pretty Spanish village or Italian lake or petite French coastal town, but you were sure to have a good time. They would be staying on the Palm at a five-star resort called Five Palm Jumeirah which had three pools, eight restaurants and a nightclub. People like Paris Hilton had stayed there so Bay's expectations were high.

The girls had rallied round, organising their lives for a holiday in the space of 48 hours. Bay was more practical, making sure she had checked the correct boxes for the dates she'd be away for her guest parking permit outside Olivia's flat and got up to speed with the articles she'd need to write out there. Sally had been surprisingly understanding. She had even encouraged Bay to produce a piece on Dubai for a travel segment. Bay could see the perks of being a freelancer, other than the tax self-return she'd have to endure if she was still, technically, working for herself in a year's time. At least for the moment, it provided her with the flexibility she needed to enjoy her new life.

Olivia, on the other hand, had been prepping herself by booking in for a session of laser hair removal, manis, pedis, a spray tan and a late-night shop for a new holiday wardrobe at Westfields shopping mall in Shepherds Bush. Bay went with her that Saturday night, a night off in Olivia's world of dinners, drinks, events and clubs. The mall was huge, and they must have clocked up a fair few miles walking around from shop to shop. There was everything imaginable in the mall from high end Louis Vuitton and Hermes to high street Zara and Topshop. There was even a Primark that was three storeys high! Olivia said that she split her wardrobe between standout designer accessories and key pieces and basics from anywhere you could get a tee shirt for under £30. After three hours, Olivia had bought a total of surprisingly just four items: a bright orange Gucci belt to stand out in Instagram pictures, a green floaty, maxi dress from Zara with big pink flowers on it, a white straw trilby hat with interchangeable coloured ties to go around the rim from Reiss and a pair of nude sandals with a small heel from Kurt Geiger that she said would go with everything.

Feeling exhausted and without anything to show for herself, Bay suggested they grab a bite to eat so they headed for a little tapas bar where they enjoyed a carafe of sangria and some patatas bravas and chicken to share.

'I'm so excited,' Bay grinned, taking another sip of sangria.

'You are? I haven't had a holiday in four months!' blurted out Olivia.

Bay was pretty sure the average Brit holidayed precisely 1.4 times a year, which meant most would go nearly ten months without so much as seeing a hotel pool.

Changing the subject, Bay asked Olivia what had been swirling around her mind all day. 'I know we were kind of joking last night, but what do you really think about Mia and the stage? Do you think it was an accident or do you think it was more sinister?'

Olivia held out her hand to admire the craftsmanship of her beauty therapist's work on her shellac-covered, bubble-gum-pink nails.

'Pfft,' she replied. 'Who's to know, but all I can say is "get me on that plane."'

They spent the remainder of the evening packing, and although Bay hadn't planned a holiday so soon, at least she wasn't short of cases. She'd barely had time to unpack over the busy last few days, so she had to unpack to repack.

'Liv, how many shoes are you taking for four days?' Bay called.

'Eleven,' replied Olivia.

'*Eleven?*' Bay sat up and headed to Olivia's room to see how she would possibly justify 11 pairs of shoes.

'Yes! Three eye-catching evening pairs, I suppose I'll have to double up one night,' she began. Bay looked at her one pair of strappy black evening shoes and thought she would be quadrupling up on her old faithfuls. Olivia continued, 'Two mid-heels for smart day, a pair of wedges, two pairs of flip flops, my new Kurt Geigers, a pair of trainers and some slippers.'

Bay didn't even own eleven pairs of shoes. Her black heels, white plimsolls, sandals and flip flops seemed plenty enough.

'So, do we have anything planned whilst we're there?' asked Bay, returning to her packing.

'Carl's organised the itinerary, but I expect there will be parties and brunches, which are a huge thing in Dubai,' Olivia stated.

'Brunches?' interrupted Bay. 'I thought you couldn't drink in Dubai.'

'Oh, bless you, naive woman. Sure you can, it's all a big con to get you to spend money on overpriced drink. Sure, you can't walk around pissed as a parrot or you'll be in the slammer and you can only buy it in designated places such as the hotels. So, everyone just travels from hotel to hotel buying glasses of wine for the equivalent of a tenner,' explained Olivia throwing a dozen or so bikinis into her case.

'I see.' Bay gulped at the hit her bank card was about to take, hoping Carl would be footing the bill for most things and they would gratefully be his obliging guests. Hopefully, the privilege of a free holiday and free booze would not mean they were indebted to return other favours. She decided to make this clear with Olivia.

'So, Liv, if Carl is paying for all of this, he's not like expecting us to be his, um, at his beck and call?'

'You mean sex slaves?' chuckled Olivia. 'God no, in Dubai you can barely get away with staying in the same room with a man unless you're married with the same surname, yet alone have an orgy with Carl Baker!' She cackled again at the thought. 'Look the guy has more money than sense and he's about to shoot a ridiculously expensive movie with a girl who nearly got blamed for murder and then nearly had a 200kg speaker land on her head. He just wants her to chill the fuck out, so she has nothing to stress her out when they begin filming next month. Simples!'

Bay guessed Olivia was right. She just had to get used to this way of life where freebies were shoved down your neck every day, and people could spend money other people had barely saved in a lifetime on a mere club night out!

They finally finished packing and rolled their suitcases out into the hallway. Bay's medium-sized, bright pink unbranded case with broken handle acting like the unruly and naughty little sister of Olivia's two large pearl-coloured roll-along Samsonites, in all their sophisticated glory with matching initialled luggage tags. They stood back to admire their hard work at packing; it was 1am and they needed to get to bed so after a cup of tea and biscuit, they went their separate ways in Olivia's flat.

The next day, Molly and Mia arrived at Olivia's at 4pm ready to leave at 5pm, to be at the airport by 6pm, two hours before their 8pm flight. Olivia lived furthest west in the direction of Heathrow which was just an hour's drive along the A40 once they got to the Hammersmith roundabout. Olivia had booked a taxi through a company called Addison Lee and a smart Ford Galaxy pulled up outside at two minutes to five, punctual and pristine. The driver was in a suit and Bay felt like they had a private chauffeur. He loaded their luggage into the back and the girls clambered in, Olivia in the front as always.

'Passports?' she called from her VIP seat.

'Yes,' responded the other three.

'Great, that's all we really need, anything else we can buy!' she bellowed from the front.

Bay fanned herself with her hand. This was already sounding like a trip she seriously wasn't going to be able to afford. She told herself not to worry as she'd watched many of her friends fly by the seat of their pants on their gap year abroad, with zero pennies to their name and no sense of a plan and they had returned in one piece. Although, she realised that was ten years ago when no-one gave a fuck or knew what they were doing or had any kind of responsibilities. Now those same people had mortgages and little ones to feed. They had taken on responsibilities by the bucketload and there was Bay, barely able to afford the mandatory daily glass of rosé with her friends let alone an entire round.

She pulled herself together quickly, reminding herself how far she had come. Yeah sure she was in her overdraft, but she had got a cushy little job in the space of three days in London. Some would wait months, having to go on the dole because of the lack of opportunities. And, hell she was flying to Dubai after just a few days in the City, all expenses paid in a five star hotel, *and* she drove all the way to London on her own without a navigator – all 250 miles of A303, M3, M25 and M4, not to mention tackling the busy London traffic head on. She nodded to herself; this was simply a reward for her hard work and nothing to worry about.

They quickly checked in their luggage and got through security at Heathrow. Instead of browsing the shops, they sat at Searcys Champagne Bar and bought a bottle to celebrate. Miraculously, the flight was running to schedule and they were soon boarding.

Looking at their tickets, Olivia asked, 'Mia, is this first class, premium economy, business?'

Mia shrugged. 'No idea,' she replied.

'I bet it's first,' Olivia squealed. Setting her already high expectations even higher, thought Bay. Their group was called, and they excitedly scampered off down the jetty leading to the plane.

'Good evening.' A pretty flight attendant greeted them with a welcoming smile.

'Hi,' replied Olivia, handing over the tickets and proceeding to turn left.

'Oh, this way, Madam, just down here on the right.' The air hostess grabbed Olivia by the shoulders, span her round and pretty much rugby tackled her off down the aisle towards row 17, economy.

'Nooo.' Olivia's groans could be heard heading off, dragging her feet to row 17. She grimaced at the already-crying babies and flinched at every sneeze or cough from one of the other people on board. 'Oh God, I didn't even pack an eye mask, as I'd been sure we'd be getting one.' She was almost in tears.

'You can have mine, Liv.' Bay selflessly pulled hers from her handbag and gave it to Olivia.

The plane was huge with two seats down one row, an aisle then four seats in the middle row, another aisle and two seats in a further row. As they were a group of four, they were sat in the middle. Olivia began looking around the floor when they arrived at row 17.

'Looking for something, Ma'am?' Another steward tried to assist.

'Yes, the leg room.' Olivia shot him a glance.

He gave a false laugh, a joke he must hear all too often, although Olivia wasn't joking. They sat down. Molly, Mia, Olivia then Bay. Each seat head had its own TV and Bay thought this was easily the most high-tech plane she'd ever been on. Looking through the movie selection, things that were still being shown in the cinema were on the list along with 500 other titles. The food menu was delicious too, with a choice of beef bourguignon, chicken salsa, fish pie and vegetarian lasagne for dinner.

The take-off was smooth, that and landing were the parts Bay feared most on a plane other than flushing the toilet. She recalled that 99% of plane accidents occurred at the very beginning or very end of a flight, she'd seen it on *Holidays from Hell*. Once they were sailing through the dimming night skyline, Bay relaxed. Olivia was already in holiday mode, a scary looking green face mask on, covered with Bay's eye mask that would now have the gooey, rejuvenating moisture all over it. An air hostess came round and took a drinks order.

'I'll have the chicken,' spurted Olivia, a little too loudly over the silencing of her headphones.

All the girls and the air hostess began laughing hysterically at the slapstick silliness of the situation. Everything was off to a great start. If only it could continue that way.

CHAPTER 19

'The City of gold.'

They touched down at DXB, Dubai's international airport. It was about 8am local time before they made it through passport control and collected their luggage. Olivia had already been told off twice by the strict security, one for wearing a hat and sunglasses and once for taking a selfie in a security queue that explicitly said, 'no phones.' She flirted with the officer by trying to play the naive ditsy girl card, but he was having none of it and pointed to a pretty straight forward picture of a phone with a big red cross through it.

'Hello Dubai! I wonder what Carl has got for us, a limo?' Olivia beamed as they exited the airport into the already-balmy morning.

Mia was reading her emails. 'Says here to look for Travel Republic,' she said, squinting in the sun.

They eventually found the Travel Republic kiosk and were directed towards a tubby, short man who resembled Danny DeVito, having a cigarette in a clearly marked 'no smoking' area. Maybe the rules here aren't as strict as they made out, thought Bay.

'He doesn't look like he drives a limo!' wailed Olivia, grabbing her hair in anger.

She was right. They followed the man as he waddled towards a silver minivan. He took their cases and threw them into the boot. Olivia kept flinching as both her initialled Samsonite cases were heaved into the van.

'My Jimmy Choos!' she wailed, trying to slow the little man down.

They boarded the bus. Olivia, who, like the others had had minimal sleep, still had the remnants of her face mask attached to her hairline and any foundation had now been wiped clean, plus the eye mask had really smudged her mascara and she resembled a heroin addict with her wide eyes and skinny face. Plus, when she realised other people were joining them on the coach, she began rocking like a mad woman.

A group of northern English women, probably on a hen party, boarded. Clearly, they had taken advantage of the free alcohol on the flight and the altitude had doubled their units as they came on laughing and messing around. One of them had a laugh worse than Olivia's. It went right through you and sounded like a baby dinosaur. Olivia rolled her eyes and popped on her oversized Victoria Beckham shades and turned her head towards the window. It didn't get any better as the group of women insisted on requesting songs for the driver to play on his sound system like he was a human jukebox and not in control of a large vehicle containing eight human lives. He was currently playing Adele's live tour recording and one of the hens was singing "Someone Like You", her accuracy clouded by the sheer volume of alcohol she had so obviously consumed.

'I'm going to kill Carl,' Olivia turned and hissed at Mia, who was sat in the seat behind her. 'Even my eighteenth in Kavos wasn't as rowdy as this.'

Bay actually thought it was lovely to see the older women, who were probably in their 40s, enjoying a girly getaway. They were clearly having fun in their own skins and weren't afraid to show it. She hoped she would be bantering with her friends on a girls' getaway like them at 40, too!

It took an hour to reach the hotel, not because of the distance but because of the traffic.

'You think London's bad!' Mia observed the standstill outside as the cars slowly crept along an eight-lane bit of motorway.

They'd been stuck in the same queue with the same outlook for the last 20 minutes so the wonder of seeing the Burj Khalifa, the world's tallest building, on the horizon no longer seemed a novelty. The sun beat down and the temperature gauge on the van was slowly creeping past 20 and it was only 9.15am. Bay had made the conscious decision, before they left, to delete her iPhone weather app as it only depressed her obsessing over the forecast which was ever-changing with each refresh. Not to the mention the fact that it was often totally wrong even in real time. Once she had been looking at a brilliant blue sky and the app had said it was cloudy! If they couldn't even get it right at the exact moment, let alone predict the future weather, Bay decided she would simply use her eyes and look out of the window every morning and dress for whatever weather she saw. She had heard from a friend that Dubai only had three days of rain a year, yet another friend had told her a group of them had flown out to watch the cricket in Dubai and it had been rained off. She had chosen to take a risk on the first friend's version of the forecast and subsequently not brought an umbrella but instead a lot of swimwear!

The van eventually pulled up outside the Five Palm Jumeirah and they were greeted by staff members in their pristine white uniforms who offered to take their luggage. The hen party was still on the bus, heading deeper out on to the Palm, their karaoke style voices following and leaving a tranquil silence behind. The doors were pulled open for the girls and they entered the hotel on marbled floors with a central water fountain grabbing their attention in the lobby. A girl carrying a tray of four champagne-based cocktails headed towards them.

'Good morning, ladies. Welcome. How was your journey?' she cooed, handing them each a glass.

'Ah, this is better.' Olivia relaxed into their five-star surroundings. The lady escorted them to the reception desk and checked them in. The men in white had already taken their luggage up to the rooms.

'So, who's sleeping with whom?' Molly asked looking at the check in information handed to them.

Olivia looked at the details probably trying to see which room was on the higher floor and had a better view. 'Oh, erm, there seems to be only one room?' she quizzed. Looking at the 1001 room key in front of her.

'Yes, you're in a two-bedroom suite,' the check in lady pointed out. The girls screamed excitedly.

Olivia flipped the room key between her thumb and forefinger, looking like she was thinking 'now this is a bit of me' and they skipped off towards the lifts. They got out on the 10th floor, only two levels below the top. Olivia flashed the magnetised key card over the button, and they were in. The whole place had cream marbled walls; it was basically an apartment. They headed down a corridor to a rectangular living room with a six-sector glass dining table to the left and a plush L-shaped sofa to the right. It was all floor-to-ceiling glass windows and a double door led out of the centre to a balcony that extended the length of the property.

The four of them rushed out into the Dubai sun, still clutching their glasses. The balcony had four sun loungers and a wooden table with a parasol. It looked out over the T-shaped pool ten storeys below and out over the water. The Burj Al Arab, the seven-star hotel shaped like a sail, could be seen just a short distance away. They took a few minutes to admire the view before heading inside to check out the bedrooms. There were two rooms, a mirror image of one another, each with an ensuite with separate shower and bath. One was on the side of the lounge and the other the dining table side. Bay was to share with Olivia and Mia with Molly.

A bottle of champagne, a fruit basket and a £1,000 voucher for the Emirates Mall, the largest shopping centre in the world, waited for them on the dining table along with a letter from Carl. Whilst Olivia popped open the bottle, Mia peeled open the letter.

She read, 'To my girls, Dubai is always a good answer and I'm glad you said 'yes'. Enjoy the stay and I'll see you all tonight at 8pm at STK. Taxi will be outside. Carl. X.'

'Cute,' said Mia, flipping over to the back in case she'd missed anything.

Creepy, thought Bay, still being overly cautious. But he hadn't done badly with the room situation and if she wedged a chair from the dining room under the main door, even if he somehow had his own key and intended creeping in during the dark of the night, he wouldn't be able to get in. The other girls might think she was rather odd but safety first! Anyway, she'd cross that bridge when it came to it.

After a long flight with little sleep and feeling slightly grubby with a long day ahead of them, the girls decided to have a couple of hours nap, then shower and see what food they could find at around midday.

Bay woke up at 11.17 am exactly to a text on her phone. It was from her ex, Henry, saying he hoped she was doing well and what was she doing in Dubai? He'd clearly seen her Instagram picture with the four of them pulling silly poses at the check in at Heathrow. She'd captioned it 'LDN to DXB – Dubai what's happening?' She didn't reply but she didn't think she wanted to or needed to. It was a refreshing feeling knowing she could stand on her own two feet, only having to think about herself, not having to worry about anyone else. She felt a sense of purpose and didn't want to waste any more of the day sleeping, so she got out of bed quietly, not wanting to wake Olivia, selected a bikini and tiptoed to the lounge. She grabbed an apple from the fruit bowl and headed out to eat it on the balcony.

The humidity hit her straight on as she exited the air-conditioned suite. She hadn't felt heat like this for a long time, as she and Henry hadn't had the money for a holiday over the last two years so they'd made do with the Cornish coastline, which was beautiful but lacked the most important holiday factor - the sun! Bay sat on one of the four wooden chairs surrounding the table outside and admired the view. The water that sat between the leaves of Palm Jumeirah sparkled in the sunlight, there wasn't a cloud in the sky and there was a joyous background noise of the clattering of plates and chit chat from the hotel restaurant two floors above. A little brown bird, the size of a robin, perched itself on the glass balcony and sang a sweet little song before becoming airborne once more.

If only humans had wings like that little bird, Amy could have soared high above the balcony and seen who had pushed her. Although there was still some specula- tion as to what had actually happened, the stories in the news still focussed on the blurry CCTV footage from the hotel which was yet to be released to the public. Bay tried to remove the sorrowful tale from her mind.

They were there to enjoy themselves and de-stress, not to dwell on the events of the last week.

Bay popped her feet up on the table and closed her eyes. She must have drifted off because the next minute she was being woken up by someone pushing her feet off the table. It was Olivia, looking slightly bedraggled, wearing one of her eleven pairs of shoes - the slippers.

'Get those hooves off the table, brunch will be arriving shortly. I took the liberty of ordering room service.' She smiled.

Bay was getting used to Olivia's brutal wit. Her rude and offensive manner was no longer something to be upset by. It simply meant she liked you and it was her way of saying 'we're friends'. The more awful she was to you, the more she liked you. Bay thought Olivia must like her a lot right now as she proceeded to mock Bay's choice of bikini.

The balcony doors rolled open once more and Mia and Molly came out, followed by two members of the concierge team dressed in cream. They wheeled in a trolley full to the brim with various breakfast options. There were little silver trays of turkey bacon, chicken sausages and tomatoes which were still simmering away omitting that delicious meaty smell. There was a pot of scrambled eggs, another of poached eggs, toast, and a stack of sweet-smelling pancakes dripping with syrup and covered in raspberries, blueberries and some sort of cream as well as a wicker basket of a mix of pastries. A huge jug of orange juice, a cafetiere of coffee and a pot of steaming tea completed the line-up.

Bay looked at the absolute feast, fit for a king, and wondered how on earth it was going to fit on the table. Luckily, the men said they'd leave the trolley and collect it later on. They had pushed it to the back against the wall like a mini buffet. Olivia had already swiped a croissant as they passed her and was now nibbling away at it, dropping pastry flakes everywhere.

They had just finished tucking into their breakfast and Bay was considering going for a second round of scrambled eggs, when the doorbell to the suite rang. The girls looked at each other wondering who it could be. Even though they had come away to try and escape the drama back home, they couldn't help but feel on edge. Bay could see the girls looked a little startled.

'Probably concierge bringing us pudding,' Olivia shrugged, trying to calm everyone down.

'Pudding for breakfast?' Molly raised her eyebrows at Olivia's attempt at a sensible explanation.

'Fine, only trying to help, you're right it's probably Amy's murderer coming to pop us all off, one by one like the *Scream* movies, starting with whoever opens the door,' Olivia teased.

Molly's expression went from sarcastic to nervous and she took a swig of orange.

The doorbell rang again, followed by a knock. The girls jumped and Olivia cackled. Mia was the one who finally gathered the courage to get up and answer the door. She tossed her napkin on the chair as she left and wiped the sticky excess of the jam from her croissant off her hands and onto the robe she was wearing.

The girls watched her cross the living room until she disappeared round the corner along the corridor to the front door. They heard the door open, followed by a shocked gasp from Mia and an, 'Oh my god, what are you doing here?'

CHAPTER 20

'Poolside Gossip' *

Bay, Mia and Olivia exchanged glances, not knowing if Mia's greeting of whoever was at the door was one of friendliness or fear. Either way she sounded surprised. Bay opened her mouth to ask who the others thought it was, but Olivia stopped her by making a 'ssh' sound and putting a finger to her lips.

It was a man's voice, but they couldn't make out the whole conversation, just Mia's high- pitched voice followed by the man's low, mumbled response.

'It doesn't sound like she's been shot in the face, so that's a good sign,' Olivia smirked, reclining onto a sun lounger with a cup of tea.

Molly giggled and her tensed body relaxed along with Olivia, realising they weren't in any immediate danger. Bay was relieved too but still wanted to find out who had come to the door, so she got up and headed inside. The cool air conditioning was surprisingly welcoming as she padded through the apartment and turned the corner to the door.

* "Poolside Gossip"; iconic colour
photograph shot by Slim Aarons, 1970

She stopped in her tracks, also surprised at who was stood chatting to Mia. It was Max, and he waved when he saw Bay. Bay gave a little wave back and forced a smile.

'Hey,' she finally managed as she kissed Max on both cheeks. 'This is a surprise, what brings you here?' she quizzed, ever the journalist.

'The house is having some work done so Dad and I thought we'd come for a little getaway to Dubai,' he explained.

'Oh, your dad's here, too?' Bay took a step back and glanced at Mia, trying to catch her eye, whilst avoiding Max's gaze.

'Yes, Michael is here too and we'll all be seeing each other later at dinner, so that's great, wonderful, in fact we can't wait, so yeah, see you at eight,' Mia said breathlessly, kissed her boyfriend on the lips and then slammed the door in his face.

With Michael Merrygold being the number one suspect to the girls in Amy's supposed murder and Mia's supposed attempted murder, it seemed the problems they were trying to escape from had followed them on a first-class flight halfway across the world.

Mia and Bay rushed back out to the balcony to update Molly and Olivia. Mia was rubbing her temple with one hand trying to add everything up.

'What the fuck are they doing here?' Olivia asked, sitting bolt upright.

'He said something about their house having some work done, right?' Bay filled in for Mia, who just nodded.

'But why here and who said they could come for dinner?' Molly squinted into the sun.

Both Mia and Bay responded with a shrug.

'Why didn't he tell you he was coming?' Olivia butted in again.

'I don't know. He said it was a surprise,' Mia replied.

'Did you find out any decent information from that conversation?' Olivia spoke like she was scolding a staff member at her work. 'And you call yourself a journalist, shame.' Olivia pointed a finger at Bay who couldn't figure out if Olivia was joking or being deadly serious.

'We'll just have to do some team investigating this evening,' Bay put in her two pennies' worth. The other three girls nodded in unison.

'So, let's get dressed and check out the pool.' Olivia got up from her sun lounger.

'I don't know if I can relax around the pool. I just don't know what to do with myself.' Mia brushed her hair behind her ears, her shoulders were drooped, and she was looking around nervously like a schoolchild before sitting an exam.

'Of course you can. Look we came here for a holiday, so naturally we'll sit around the pool and soak up this beautiful weather. Pick up a Cosmo and you'll soon forget about everything. For all we know, we could be worrying about nothing. Sure, some odd things have happened, but it could just be a coincidence and we've put two and two together and made a million.' This was probably the most logical thing Olivia had ever said, and although Bay still needed some convincing, she nodded in optimistic support of her friend.

Mia seemed to calm down as she too nodded, before saying, 'Thanks, Liv, I needed to hear something like that. So, let's go and work on our tan lines and did you mean Cosmo, the magazine, or the drink?'

'Both!' smiled Olivia.

The girls raced around the apartment finding their most skimpy bikini to get the best tan and flinging on a cover-up over it. Always feeling like the sensible mother of the group, Bay packed a beach bag with sun cream and water.

'Ready?' she called into the living area.

'Ready,' responded the others.

They headed down to the pool, visiting the little hotel shop in the lobby on the way to collect a selection of magazines to read. Unfortunately, there were only two sun loungers left together so Mia and Olivia took them whilst Bay and Molly headed to the pool bar to grab a drink. With Molly's very pale skin, she wasn't one to sit baking in the sun anyway. They hopped up on to the high bar stools at a tall round table and ogled over the extensive cocktail list and bar snacks. Bay hadn't spent much alone time with Molly, so was looking forward to getting to know her better.

After taking advantage of the two-for-one cocktails and now three pina coladas down and trying to deal with jet lag, they were soon feeling a little tipsy.

'So, how are things with Archie after everything?' Bay plucked up the courage to move the conversation on from lowbrow topics such as clothes and London brunch spots to something a little deeper.

'Yeah, all good, so awkward at first though. Oh my God, when you guys left, he was devastated that we thought he had pushed Amy, more so than the fact he'd kept his trading debt a secret.' Molly gave a little laugh as she swayed slightly in her seat.

That was the most Bay had ever heard Molly talk and she admired her easy-going nature. Although the girl could be quite naive and ditsy sometimes, she was kind and carefree and had actually made some valid points along the way. Bay thought her silliness was maybe more of an act she put on.

They spoke more about boys and Bay opened up about Henry and how he had texted her that morning and how she knew that she was over him. Molly went a little quiet. Bay could tell she was thinking about something else. As lovely as she was, the poor thing was useless at multi-tasking.

'All right there? Are those pina coladas getting to you?' Bay laughed, waving at Molly's face.

'Oh, ha, yeah, Sorry,' Molly did her trademark girly giggle. 'Can I tell you something, if you swear you won't tell the others?'

Bay pushed her sunglasses back up her nose where they had slid down like a slide with the amount of sun cream she had applied. She didn't want Molly to see her eyes as she didn't know the outcome of her reaction to Molly's upcoming confession.

'Sure,' Bay smiled a friendly smile that implied 'your secret is safe with me.'

'I think Mia is cheating on Max.' Molly was straight to the point, with none of her usual fluffiness.

Bay's eyes widened as she once again pushed her sunglasses back up her nose. This was not the silly bit of side gossip Molly normally produced when she tried to get involved in Olivia's dramatic dropping of celebrity bombshells. This was big, particularly given the current circumstances.

'What do you mean? Why do you think that?'

'When we went to bed this morning, she was up texting all the time. Her phone kept bleeping so I couldn't really get to sleep. I assumed it was Max, but I now know he would have been on a plane and she had no idea he was even coming so they couldn't have spoken.' Molly sucked at the straw of her empty cocktail glass, looking like she was desperately trying to get any remaining juice.

'Umm. Hmm. Right, but it could have been Max though, you know, they've got Wi-Fi on planes nowadays,' Bay added, trying to find an explanation.

'They do?' Molly looked puzzled and then a little embarrassed that she could possibly have been wrong about her best friend's infidelity.

'Yeah, I think so, particularly on long haul flights,' Bay shrugged.

'Oh well. What about when she wouldn't let us read that text from Bachelor Ben?' Molly persisted.

'Oh yeah,' was all Bay could manage. How could she have let the three pina coladas (which were probably watered down significantly) cloud her brain? She suddenly remembered the first night out in Kensington when she'd been queuing for the bathroom and accidently spotted Mia and Bachelor Ben together in a private room, and she recalled the way Ben was flirting with her on the red carpet at the hotel. Molly was right about Mia not letting them see the texts on her phone, too. It did kind of all add up, but Bachelor Ben was engaged now, and he and Mia would be starring together in the film, so they did have the right to be chatting together.

Her thoughts were interrupted by a fracas coming from the pool area. Bay wasn't surprised to see Olivia caught up in the middle of it. It looked as though she'd said something to Mia who was now stomping off towards the hotel lobby. She hadn't even stopped to put her shoes on. Olivia turned round to face Molly and Bay at the pool bar, and she stood shaking her head.

Molly and Bay looked at each other and Bay jumped off her seat ready to head over to Olivia. She was stopped by Molly, who grabbed her arm.

'Hey, don't say anything about the Mia/Bachelor Ben thing,' she whispered.

Bay patted Molly's hand which was still attached to her arm. 'Of course not,' she replied.

'Babe, what did you say?' Molly asked, as she reached Olivia at her sunbathing spot.

'What? Me? Nothing!' Olivia looked slightly sheepish like a dog when it knew it had done something bad.

Although Bay's sunglasses were now stuck firmly to her nose, Olivia must have still been able to read the 'bullshit' expression on her face as she explained. 'No, seriously, I asked to read her magazine because I'd finished mine and thought we could swap but she said 'no' so I said 'what?, is there some horrific picture of you with no make-up on or have you been caught doing something you shouldn't be?' She just looked at me, huffed and puffed like the big, bad wolf and then stormed off.'

Molly and Bay exchanged glances again, after the conversation they had just had, they could almost put money on what Mia had read in that magazine. Someone had found out about her and Ben and printed it.

'Which magazine?' asked Bay.

'I don't know. What? What is it? You two know something, don't you?' Olivia stared at them over the frame of her sunglasses.

Bay and Molly dashed off towards the lobby, leaving Olivia frantically cramming her life back into her tiny Gucci pouch belt.

'Wait!' yelled Olivia, collecting her things into her arms. 'Don't leave me in the dark, I can't be last to know a secret.' She began running desperately after Bay and Molly, flip flopping loudly on the poolside tiles. She caught up with them in the lobby supermarket where they were flicking through the pages of various magazines. Olivia joined in.

'What are we looking for?' she questioned, shooting side glances between the magazine and the girls.

'Bingo!' cried Bay shaking out a magazine.

'Let me see, let me see!' Olivia barged Molly out of the way in desperation to read a story that for once in her PR career, she didn't already know.

Bay showed her the small picture in the left-hand corner of page 32 of the brunette and Bachelor Ben. Olivia snatched the magazine from Bay and her jaw dropped as she let her factor six sun accelerator fall out of under her arm and to the floor.

'Bachelor Ben and Amy!' she said in shock.

'Amy?' Bay gave Molly a confused glance, she yanked the magazine back from Olivia who was still processing the information.

Bay read the small 'Z' list article to herself.

Socialite and actress Amy Braybury who fell to her death at a party last week was hiding a secret. The brunette was having an affair with the actor nicknamed Bachelor Ben, although he is now engaged. Ben is soon to be starring alongside Amy's arch-rival Mia Bonaventura in The Trouble With Us, *the highly anticipated film by Carl Baker set for release next year.*

CHAPTER 21

**'Better to be slapped by the
truth than kissed with a lie.'**

The three of them returned to room 1001, but there was no sign of Mia, even though they had tried calling her multiple times. They sat in the lounge. Although the sun was still beating down on the balcony, they decided the excess heat had made them all a little bit mad and they needed to focus.

Bay and Molly had decided to 'spill the beans' on their theory of Mia being involved with Bachelor Ben. Olivia summarised the situation as she scribbled into a Five Palm Jumeirah branded notebook. 'So, Bachelor Ben was up to his old tricks and had Amy as his side thing and potentially our friend too, although we are yet to hear it from the horse's mouth. Someone has leaked the Amy and Ben thing to the press, so where does that leave everything?' she asked, looking blankly at the others.

'I guess it makes Ben our new suspect, he wanted to end it with Amy but maybe she had too much against him and his new goody-two-shoes image, so he needed to get rid of her,' Molly suggested.

'It's certainly a possibility and if it is true about him and Mia, he'd do anything to keep that under wraps too, by trying to get rid of her!' continued Bay.

'Where the hell is she?' Olivia hung up her phone after trying to reach Mia for the hundredth time.

As she did so, the apartment door flung open and in walked Mia.

'Take a seat,' Olivia demanded, standing up and offering her chair.

Mia sat obediently and put her head in her hands.

'Tell us everything,' Olivia ordered.

Mia looked up with a blank expression.

'Look, we know about Ben and Amy, we saw the magazine,' Bay explained.

'Urgh,' growled Mia, knowing she was cornered.

'So why were you so upset about the Ben article in the magazine?' Olivia pushed for answers, but Mia stayed silent.

'Look, we're only worried about you because Ben could now be a potential suspect,' sympathised Bay.

'No, it wasn't him.' Mia broke her silence.

'But it makes sense if they were an item and he lost interest but knew she had too much on him, which would finish his career.' Olivia presented their theory.

'No, Liv, he wasn't there,' Mia's voice got louder.

'Where was he then?' Olivia held her arms out for an answer.

Mia sighed. 'He was with me,' she revealed, sitting back in the chair and looking up at the ceiling. 'When I got in the lift and you guys were in it, I was coming back from his room. That's why it was so awkward when we bumped into him and Carl on the ground floor.'

'Oooh,' chimed the other three girls together.

'Ew,' added Olivia, 'You and Ben?' She made a suggestive hand signal.

'Oh My God, no! I never did anything, I swear. But he was all over me saying he could make me a star and I was so desperate to make it as a serious actress that I just thought some harmless flirting might catapult me to the next level! I can't let Max find out. His dad would kill me if Max didn't first.'

'Wrong choice of words, Mia!' Olivia grimaced.

'Yeah, you don't need to say anything to anyone right now. Have a conversation with Ben when you get back and take it from there. Sure, he might not have pushed Amy himself, but I think we should be wary of the guy.' Bay got up to top up her glass with water from the mini-fridge.

'I'll talk to him tonight.' Mia got up too.

'Tonight?' Molly's puzzled face returned.

'Yeah, Carl flew Ben out to Dubai too. I knew that already, but I didn't want to make a big deal of it.' Mia put her hands on the oversized dining table and stretched like a cat.

'What! I can't believe I'm the last to know all of these things. I'm losing my talent for obtaining gossip!' Olivia seemed genuinely disappointed with herself.

LEXIE CARDUCCI

'This is going to be an interesting night for sure!' Bay sipped at her fresh glass of cold water.

'I'm quite looking forward to it!' Olivia had perked up again.

'Mmmm, well. Let's see what happens. I just want to have a good night and put all this crap on the back burner! So, what else is in that minibar? Something stronger than water, I hope!' Mia shook out her hair, also seeming to be in a better mood.

Olivia turned on some cheesy pop music which blasted from the built-in speaker system and glass after glass of champagne was poured whilst getting ready for the evening ahead. Every girl knows that getting ready is the best part of the evening. Taking it in turns to parade around the living room in a shortlist of favourite outfits and cheering each other on. Mia showed off a mix of hilarious dance moves and mock catwalk poses on the makeshift dance floor before her outfit was chosen for her. Bay followed, feeling a little self-conscious. Molly strutted down and even attempted a cartwheel that nearly had her end up knocking ornaments off a sideboard and Olivia offered up some sort of break dance move.

Bay chose a high-waist pair of pink flares that had a matching pink bandeau top for Molly. Olivia had a long black silk slip dress with a huge slit up one side, a feather choker necklace and a bright Marilyn Munroe red lipstick. For Bay, the girls voted for a gold sequin mini dress with a 'V' neckline and long sleeves with 80s style shoulder pads. Molly had pulled Bay's auburn hair

-187-

back into a slick pony. Last but not least was Mia, who had disagreed with the other girls' favourite choice which was a leopard print ruffle midi dress and opted for her own personal winner which was a short red jumpsuit with a t-shirt style top with buttons down. Mia let her hair fall down in loose curls.

Bay joined the line-up on the balcony, ready to leave for the restaurant and snapped a few quick selfies and pictures before leaving.

It was a refreshing atmosphere, Bay thought, as they hopped in the blacked-out Mercedes waiting for them outside the hotel. It was as if they had been transported back to before the night of Amy's death, when they were just four carefree city girls who drank rosé far too early in the day than deemed acceptable and put on garments they couldn't afford before going on nights out to places they also, more than likely, couldn't afford.

Here they were now, off to another lavish restaurant-cum-bar-cum-club because when you're a super cool place like STK, why not offer all three under one roof? They pulled up outside a tall skyscraper in the vicinity of Dubai Marina. There was already a queue of stylish-looking girls on the arms of handsome men, most wearing skin tight white jeans and some sort of moccasins on their feet.

Mia texted Carl on the way to say they would be there in ten minutes and he'd replied to say that he'd be waiting outside. Sure enough, there he was, although he was looking very different from the other times Bay had seen him. He'd had his fluffy overgrown grey hair cut back into a stylish silver fox do ala George Clooney and his weird blacked out sunglasses that resembled ski goggles had been replaced by a rather fancy looking pair of circular tortoiseshell Tom Ford glasses. He was looking like a very dapper gentleman indeed!

Olivia had clearly spotted the man's new found attractiveness too as she applied an extra spritz of perfume from a mini diffuser canister she had in her clutch bag and livened up her hairdo to such an extent that she was at a risk of it going full Amy Winehouse style beehive. She trotted over to Carl like a *Real Housewife* who smelt the opportunity to stir up some drama and held out her hand to greet him. He took it and kissed it lightly, like they did in the old fashioned black and white movies. If he had been wearing a top hat, he surely would have tipped that too! He then whisked Olivia off by her hand to one side, like some sort of tango move, before letting her go, much to Olivia's surprise as she kept on spinning, narrowly missing a wall.

After discarding Olivia to one side, Carl proceeded to hug Mia before she introduced him to Bay and Molly with a series of 'hellos,' and 'how are you,' followed by a chorus of 'thank yous,' from the girls.

Carl turned on his heels and led them through into STK, the letters of the restaurant displayed in gold above the door. Olivia was first to follow him and mimed the grabbing of Carl's perky bottom behind him whilst winking at the girls.

'You little ho!' giggled Molly.

'Yeah, you do realise that we will be on camera, Liv, and it's probably worthy of an arrest on Dubai soil?' Mia said, shaking her head at her friend's silly joke whilst cracking a cheeky smile indicating that she definitely found it hilarious.

They walked past the hostess at the bottom of the internal steps up to the dining area. The staircase and walls were all black tiles, with small flecks of silver bits in that made them sparkle. There was a strong aroma of incense wafting through the air and the loud music could be heard thumping away on the floor above, getting louder with every step they ascended.

The bass line rippled through Bay's body, shaking her insides about and probably creating a cocktail of the alcohol she'd consumed throughout the day. She was thankful they were about to eat and as Carl had splashed out on flights, a tenth-floor suite and a taxi to this place, she really hoped he wasn't about to skimp on the food.

As they walked through the double doors to gain entry, it was like walking into a circus. Bay ducked as two fire breathers on stilts shot out flames above their heads. Carl was babbling to Olivia, completely oblivious to the fire hazard directly in front of him like it was the most normal thing in the world. There was a busy bar on the left-hand side with bar staff dressed smartly in black suits, white shirts and red bow ties. The alcohol selection behind the bar was rather extensive, with every liquor you could imagine. One of the bar staff was setting fire to a marshmallow on top of a milkshake-style cocktail with what looked like a blow torch, whilst another shook a metal cocktail shaker vigorously to the rhythm of the music.

It was all very showy, and Bay could easily see why it was such a popular venue. On the right were circular tables of two, four or six, all with electric lamps in the centre and behind them was a large, square, raised stage containing the DJ, a disco ball and big speakers with more tables on the other side. Carl led them around the bar to the left and into a private section of raised tables for large groups, looking directly at the stage.

The four girls and Carl were last to arrive and took their seats to the left-hand side. The other guests included Max and Michael Merrygold, Bachelor Ben and his fiancée, and two people who, Bay supposed, worked for Carl. Molly slid in next to Bachelor Ben's fiancée, Bay presumed so as not to make it awkward for Mia. Bay sat down next to her and Mia went to grab the chair next to Carl but was beaten to it by Olivia who threw her body down so fast that if it had been a game of musical chairs, she would probably have set a new world record. Olivia celebrated her win by sticking her tongue out at Mia, before resting her hand on her left arm and turning herself round to face Carl, to finish where they had left off their conversation about nudity in film. Bay was surprised to see Bachelor Ben's fiancée there, considering the stories swirling in the papers.

Mia finally sat down between Bay and Olivia, almost directly opposite Max. The couple smiled at each other across the table. Sensing the slight awkwardness from

Mia's end, Bay thought she would jump in to ease the conversation.

'So, Max, you said your house was having some work done?' she asked, breezily, as she took a plate of crispy fried calamari that had arrived at the table along with other tapas style dishes. She took a spoonful and plopped them on her plate before passing them to her right to Mia.

'Yes, well, Dad and I think someone may have broken in so we're having a new security system installed,' explained Max, taking a sip from his beer. Michael Merrygold seemed to nod in agreement, obviously listening.

Mia dropped the spoon for the calamari onto the black tiled floor and it landed with a loud clatter. Both her and Bay bent down to pick it up, bumping heads on the way down.

'Fuck,' said Mia.

'Sorry,' replied Bay patting Mia's head.

'No, not my head! They know about us being in their house,' Mia whispered in a panic.

'Oh,' Bay whispered back as she returned to an upright position. She cleared her throat before quizzing Max some more.

'No way, really, why do you think that?' she asked coolly trying once again to sound conversational rather than crazy.

'Someone tried to access files on one of the computers and even though they somehow managed to get in with face ID, the stupid system failed to store a picture or even make them clarify who they were. You know how they are supposed to ask a security question if there's suspicious activity, like your first cat's name or the last letter of your mum's second husband's cousin's twice removed surname!' Michael Merrygold seemed rather angry as he explained the situation through a mouth full of calamari.

'All right, Dad, calm down.' Max passed his father his beer. 'We think we know who it is, anyway.' He turned to face the girls before winking at Mia.

CHAPTER 22

'Confessions on a nightclub dancefloor.'

'They know, they know!' wailed Mia, pacing up and down in the bathroom of STK. They had successfully finished dinner without bringing up any more about the security installation at the Merrygolds or anything about Amy or anything remotely suspicious or murder related at all; which was quite a triumph over the course of two hours, bearing in mind those present at the dinner table.

'Calm down and drink up,' cooed a rather drunk Olivia, picking up Mia's glass of champagne and thrusting it towards the brunette's face. Mia batted it away like it was a persistent wasp as Olivia continued to slosh the liquid all over the sinks not to mention the floor. It rolled over the edges quite easily as it was a traditional champagne coupe rather than a stemmed glass and before long there was barely anything left in it at all. Olivia noticed the lack of champagne bubbling in the glass and lifted it up closer to her eyes to peer in and double check after realising it was indeed bone dry.

She held it to the ceiling before announcing, 'This glass was based on Marie Antoinette's boob!' She cupped the glass to her own enhanced breast. 'The girl had great tits,' she concluded before placing the glass back on the countertop and leaning on the basin for support.

The other three girls ignored the drunk Olivia who was now singing Gloria Gaynor's 'I Will Survive' in a slightly sadistic tone.

'Maybe Max and his dad are completely off the trail and think it was someone else, someone Michael works with or something,' reasoned Molly, folding her arms.

'I don't think so. Did you see the way he winked at me like it was almost a warning?' Mia pulled herself up to sit on the countertop.

The toilet flushed in the end cubicle. Bay looked at Mia and whispered, 'I didn't think anyone else was in here?'

Mia shrugged. The toilet door opened which shocked the already wobbly Olivia so much that she slipped and ended up drawing a line of red lipstick up her cheek. It was Kristen, Bachelor Ben's fiancée. She smiled at the girls as she washed her hands under the taps, taking care not to get any soap stuck to the huge glistening diamond rock on her finger.

'What a cool place, dontcha think?' she said, in passing conversation as she made her way to the hand drier, dodging Olivia as she went.

'Yeah, love it!' Molly answered with a smile.

'I'll see you back on the dance floor,' Kristen sang, as she strutted back out of the ladies' room like a skinny catwalk model.

'Oh. For God's sake, you don't think she heard any of that?' Mia asked, falling against the mirrored wall at the back of the sinks.

'I doubt it. I think the only thing she would have heard was Olivia's lovely rendition of "I Will Survive."' Bay looked over at Olivia who had lipstick smeared all over her face. Now that the attention had been brought back to her, Olivia grasped the opportunity to be centre stage and in the spotlight by doing a weird little dance, shimmying towards her friends who couldn't help but burst out laughing at her cheesy jazz hands.

'I think it's time to take Roxy Hart home,' breathed Molly through fits of laughter.

Mia stopped laughing, suddenly. 'Hey, I just thought, you don't think Kristen has anything to do with this do you? What if she found out about Ben and Amy and now Ben and me?'

Molly and Bay were silent for a minute mulling over the possibility.

'No, I don't think Kristen is that aware of anything. She seems pretty oblivious to most things,' Molly said finally. 'I mean I was sat next to her tonight and had to ask multiple times for her to pass me the meatballs. I literally had to nudge her before she took any notice.

'Yeah, fair point. When I was chatting to her about their summer plans, she said how much she was looking forward to their Spanish holiday to Rome!' Bay raised her eyebrows as she retold the story.

'Rome's in Italy, not Spain,' spat Olivia, wading in on the conversation. The girls were impressed by Olivia's ability to distinguish Italy from Spain despite the state she was in.

After deciding it was rather unlikely that someone who thought Rome was in Spain could plan (let alone get away with) murder, they firmly ruled out any involvement by Kristen. In fact, by the look of how lovey dovey she was with Ben that evening it seemed as though she hadn't even read the tabloids about Ben and Amy and was none the wiser.

'She might not be geographically savvy, but in case she heard us and loves a good old gossip, which as she works in TV production, she probably has scandal for breakfast; we might want to tell Max it was us who went snooping through his computers.' Bay knew that they would have to come clean soon. Mia's face went gloomy and Bay tried to think more positively. 'To be fair, we weren't snooping. It was actually a complete accident that we stumbled across that letter,' Bay reminded Mia that they had, in fact, done nothing wrong and had simply been printing Mia's contract.

After making Olivia look presentable by removing the smudged lipstick, smoothing down her hair and giving her a mint, the group decided it was safe to re-join the others while Mia grabbed Max for a conversation.

Mia and Max headed to the bar, leaving Molly, Bay and Olivia on the dance floor with the others. Bachelor

Ben and Kristen were grinding on each other, which Bay thought was rather vulgar, so decided to turn her back on them. Michael Merrygold looked as though he was in an awkward conversation with Carl's two colleagues who had definitely taken advantage of the free booze and were being loud and quite boisterous, and Carl himself was chatting up a couple of girls who were wearing more make-up than the entire Kardashian family on a night out at the Met Gala. They clearly knew who he was and wanted to steal the chance to get their 'big break'.

Bay decided to go and support Mia at the bar with Max and left Molly and Olivia to bop along to the music.

'Do you like Dubai then?' asked Max pulling up a chair for Mia and another for Bay when he saw her heading over. Mia and Bay sat down, and Max passed a drinks menu to read.

'Oh my God I love it. I think I could move here you know. Good food, great vibes and only three days of rain a year!' Mia repeated the bit of Dubai fact that Bay had told her earlier.

'You know it gets to, like, 45 degrees in the summer though, right?' Max grinned as he tried to get the attention of a passing barman.

'Phew,' was all Mia managed in response

Bay was thinking about how to tell Max that herself, her friends and even his girlfriend suspected his dad of murder.

As Max was about to open his mouth to say something, Mia cut him short and put her hand on his leg.

'Look, there's something I want to tell you.'

Max looked at the hand on his leg and then directly at Mia and then to Bay. Bay swallowed and wished she'd ordered a drink as she was in real need of liquid courage. She gave a nod of confidence to Mia.

'OK. Well, remember when I went to yours to print my contract for the film?' Mia began.

'No,' Max replied solemnly.

Bay wasn't surprised that Max didn't remember as he never seemed to listen to anything anyone said, but now was not the time for bickering over who said what.

'I needed to print it and grab some stuff from yours, so I thought I'd use your printer. Bay drove me over and we couldn't figure out the computers and Bay somehow managed to get into one and it just started printing,' Mia explained, making it fairly to the point and straightforward.

'And what did it print?' Max sat bolt upright.

Mia needn't have answered the question. It was clear to Bay that Max knew what was on that bit of paper as he let out a big sigh. He also didn't look too angry or upset for someone who had just found out their father was a potential suspect in a murder case.

Finally, he spoke. 'Babe, it wasn't my dad who wrote that letter.' He looked her straight in the eye once more, but this time a little more assertively than before. 'It was me.'

CHAPTER 23

'Not sure if this is a hang-over, hunger or death.'

Although Bay had been quite merry the night before, and only returned to the hotel after 2am, she felt rather fresh in the morning. Unlike Olivia, who was absolutely hanging. No surprise, after her behaviour the previous night. Bay was surprised they had managed to make it to breakfast outside on the main restaurant terrace by 10am and were preparing for a feast, before a pool party that afternoon which Carl had invited them to. Olivia was hiding her hung over state well, behind oversized black shades and a pretty floral headband, plus a water bottle that had been attached to her hand all night long which seemed to be helping her through, one cold sip at a time.

Mia had requested a table outside on the terrace as Bay had learned she didn't like to waste a minute out of the sunlight. Her Italian olive skin could handle the sun's rays whereas Bay couldn't quite manage the heat, and not to mention Olivia in her fragile state.

'Phew,' breathed Bay, overcome by the dry heat. 'I think I'll go and grab some sun cream and when I get back you can tell us what happened with Max.'

'Oh babe, could you get me some paracetamol if you're going back to the room? I'm dying over here.' Olivia wiped her forehead as she pleaded for help recovering.

'I thought you were the queen of dealing with hang-overs, you must have one most days,' Mia laughed.

'It must be the Dubai alcohol, they probably have some extra strong brands from the Emirates,' Olivia puffed, now fanning herself with her hand.

'As alcohol is pretty much illegal in the Emirates, I doubt that,' Mia laughed again.

Olivia pretended to laugh too. 'Oh ha ha ha, I'll remember this next time you can't move from the sofa when you stay at mine and demand I make you a hang-over smoothie! I might accidently put salt in it and not sugar. Now, Bay, don't stand there all day, are you going to go or am I going to have to get concierge to bring me my paracetamol?'

'Yes, right, going – and don't talk about last night until I get back,' Bay called, heading back inside towards the lifts.

She yawned as she waited for the lift to arrive, feeling far too tired to take the stairs just two floors down to the room. When the lift finally came, and she'd reached her floor she tapped the electronic card to 1001 and pushed open the door. She thought she heard something fall to the floor with a thud and a door shut as she headed in. She stopped to listen again but heard nothing more and decided it must have been the fuzzy white noise often throbbing round one's head after a night out. Either that or it was room service. She headed down the internal corridor and peered into her room, the bed was still unmade and her clothing options for the day's outfits were still sprawled across the floor – it definitely wasn't room service.

Bay headed into the living room, where there was a white packet of paracetamol on the glass dining table.

Well, that was easy, she thought, picking them up. She stopped when she saw a bottle of water on the floor and wondered how on earth it got there, before picking that up as well and putting it on the table. She flinched as she thought she saw something move on the balcony but after looking again presumed it must have been the roller blind moving in the slight wind, although that was odd because the wind was coming from the open balcony door. She didn't think it was left open when they went out for breakfast, because Olivia was always complaining that it got too hot inside and that the air conditioning wouldn't work properly with the door open.

Now feeling slightly on edge, Bay tiptoed over and pulled the door to, only briefly scanning the balcony, afraid of what, or who she might see. She then rushed back through the living room, grabbed her sun cream from the messy floor in her room and ran speedily out of the door. She didn't stop running until she reached the 12th floor, two floors up, and had even taken the stairs this time as she didn't want to hang around waiting for the lift. She reached the entrance to the restaurant and shuddered. She tried to shake off the anxious feeling that someone was watching her, and she could have been seconds from being in the wrong place at the wrong time. It was the fear of the unknown and the 'what if.'

Rushing back over to the breakfast table where Molly and Mia were laughing at something and Olivia looked like she was asleep, Bay pulled out her chair and sat down quickly. She must have looked shocked because Molly stopped laughing and asked, 'What's up?'

'Did we leave the balcony door open?' asked Bay, leaning her elbows on the table.

'Oh, for goodness sake.' Olivia awoke like a dragon breathing fire at the possibility of her air-conditioned suite being contaminated by the hot desert air. 'What did I tell you all about that bloody door?' She scanned the other three girls' faces, looking for a sign of the culprit.

'No, no, we definitely shut it,' confirmed Molly.

'Yeah, Molly and I joked about not wanting to risk the wrath of a hung over Olivia.' Mia backed up Molly's story and Molly chuckled.

'Why?' asked Olivia, bluntly, as she grabbed the paracetamol from Bay.

'It was still open when I got back and I felt kind of weird, like someone else was there...' Bay trailed off at the end of her sentence as she didn't want to risk sounding stupid.

'Room service?' asked Molly.

'Nope.' Bay shook her head. 'The place is still a mess.'

'Was there anything else odd?' asked Mia.

'Only a water bottle that was on the floor, and I thought I heard something, too, when I walked in.'

Olivia rudely interrupted the conversation like she normally did when she wasn't really paying attention to anyone else. 'I know I can be a little bitch when I'm hung over, but you don't need to go putting me to sleep, Bay,' and with that she threw the paracetamol packet back at Bay.

'Sorry?' questioned Bay picking up the pack that had bounced off her chest and on to the floor.

'So you should be, my head is literally about to fall off!'

'No, stupid, she means "sorry" as in "what the fuck are you talking about?"' Mia jumped to Bay's defence.

'Sleeping pills. The girl's trying to put me to sleep for the day looking at the strength of those things.' Olivia adjusted her hair band.

'What?' Mia grabbed the pack from Bay. 'Who brought these with them? And how on earth did you get them through security, these are seriously strong?' She looked round at the girls for answers, but they all had equally bemused expressions on their faces. 'Are you telling me these don't belong to any of you?'

Bay shook her head after realising the possibility that someone had potentially been in their apartment and was planning to drug them. She got to her feet and the others followed.

'What? Where are we going? And what about break-fast?' moaned Olivia, slowly getting to her feet to avoid a head rush.

Mia took Olivia's hand and tugged her in the direction of the lift. They brushed past a waiter carrying a tray of food.

'My eggs Benedict,' Olivia wailed, seeing her break-fast waft straight by under her nose. 'Can it be sent down to 1001?' she yelled across the restaurant, before being bundled into the lift.

They entered room 1001, clambering over each other to get in quickly. They each took a room to search for anything suspicious or out of place apart from Olivia, who plonked herself down on the sofa and curled into a little ball.

'Where's the water you were on about?' Mia called to Bay from the living room.

Bay came out of her bedroom and looked around the table for it before her eyes fell on Olivia who had picked up the bottle and was unscrewing the lid ready to take a sip.

'No!' yelled Mia rushing over and removing the bottle from Olivia's clutches.

Olivia looked ready to explode with anger. Her face was screwed up and she kept opening and closing her mouth like a baby bird wanting to be fed. Bay couldn't tell whether she was going to cry or shout the roof off or both, but she didn't wait to find out. She quickly diffused the situation. 'Liv, don't you see, someone was in here and they were going to put those sleeping tablets in our water and I must have come in and disturbed them.'

'What did they plan to do once they drugged us to sleep?' Molly asked quietly.

'Well, they weren't going to put us to bed and read us a good night story, were they? Whatever their plan was, it wasn't going to end well for us.' Olivia told the facts that no-one wanted to hear.

'So, who is it then? Mia, what happened with telling Max about his dad?' Bay asked trying to piece together the clues.

'You won't believe this, but it was *Max* who wrote that letter. He never sent it, though, and he wrote it out of anger one night when he knew how much his dad would lose on the property deal that Richard Braybury screwed him over with.' Mia explained her conversation with Max at the bar.

'So, what - you believe that, and think that rules Michael out of this whole thing?' Molly quizzed, worrying that their only theory was disappearing out of the window.

Mia shrugged. 'I guess he could be lying to protect his dad?' It was more of a question than a statement.

'Or they could be in it together,' Olivia added, somewhat unhelpfully.

As the girls were processing the new information, Molly's phone buzzed. She looked at it, her eyes widening. 'Um, girls...' she said, slowly, turning the phone round so that everyone could see the screen. 'They've released the CCTV footage from the night.'

CHAPTER 24

'In Gucci we put our trust.'

The four girls sat on the sofa for over 30 minutes reviewing the footage over and over again. Olivia nodded off to sleep after the first viewing and was now snoring like a walrus.

'There's nothing here that I recognise.' Molly sounded as frustrated as the rest of them felt after viewing the 15 second clip once more.

The camera showed the mass movement of people from the hotel atrium to the suite where the speeches were given and the camera being pushed by someone who was out of sight, to face the floor. Then as they all cleared, a person in white trainers exited the door to the balcony where Amy was left only to return a few seconds later.

'Pfft,' huffed Olivia, who had just woken up and was peering over Molly's shoulder. 'Can't be anyone that important if they're wearing fake Gucci.' She laughed as she mocked the shoes on the screen.

'Ha, trust you to be repulsed by someone's fake branded shoes,' scoffed Mia.

'How do you know they're fake?' asked Molly, rewinding the video and zooming in on the shoes.

'Because they've got black lines and not green ones and the logo looks weird,' Olivia pointed out on the bit of paused footage. Although the image was blurred you could certainly tell the lines were black and not green, trust Olivia to home in on the designer logos.

'Oh my God, that's it!' yelled Bay, jumping to her feet with excitement. 'We need to find the person who's got the fake Gucci's. Are they men's or women's shoes, Liv?'

'Unisex,' replied Olivia to a reaction of disappointed faces from the girls. 'Although not many people are stupid enough to buy fake shoes that look utterly ridiculous and nothing like the real thing.'

Bay really couldn't see much difference and apparently neither could Mia or Molly, so Olivia was to be in charge of spotting *the fake monstrosities* (her words exactly), at the pool party later.

'So, once we match the shoes up to their owner, then what's the plan?' asked Molly. Bay followed her stare out of the floor-to-ceiling windows to a view of the sea sparkling in the sunlight.

The girls were so chuffed with the fact they had made a mini-breakthrough that they hadn't thought about what happens next. The evidence thus far was the letter from either Max or Michael, which after last night may or may not be relevant at all and the fact that the killer was at the hotel party, the flower show and now apparently in Dubai. Everything really was riding on matching the shoes to their owner.

The pool party was at another venue further onto the Palm, so the girls had hopped into an Uber to take them there. The building wasn't a huge glass skyscraper like most of the structures in Dubai, each trying to outdo one another with height and shape but was more of a boutique style, like a traditional Arabian villa fit for a king.

The place itself was set on one of the Palm Islands' leaves that sprouted out into the ocean from the trunk of the palm. It was clearly a very fancy area as there was a security check at the start of the road where everyone had to show ID, including the taxi driver and what could only be described as 'a mirror on a stick' was trailed around the underneath of the car, presumably checking for drugs, weapons or stowaways.

It made Bay feel a little more at ease knowing that everyone attending the pool party would have been vigorously searched for any form of illegal items. Security could not have done any more unless resorting to full body searches. As they drove along the road, which was covered in a thin layer of sand typical of most surfaces in Dubai, Bay realised two things. One was that security needed to be so tight as the houses here were from another world, they were humongous and two, it was no wonder that the Palm Jumeirah could be seen from space as it took a good ten minutes to drive along this one road.

They eventually pulled up outside the villa, which was just as stunning as the others they had passed on their way. It was a pristine, white stone building with a curved centre piece, bordered by Roman-style pillars each side of the entrance. Above that was a small pillared balcony, matching the curve of the entrance below. To each side were the wings of the house displaying four large windows to the left and a mirror image on the right. The roof was tiled with curved terracotta tiles, giving the place an almost Mediterranean feel.

The girls entered through the open black wrought iron gates and up the winding tarmac driveway, lined with lush palm trees, past a stone water fountain with a unicorn in the centre, spouting water from its rainbow-painted horn and up to the front door. They paused for a moment and looked back down the driveway in all its spectacular quirkiness like something out of Alice in Wonderland. Mia rang the doorbell. The mahogany double doors swung open and the four of them were greeted by a tall, slim brunette girl who must have been at least six foot tall. It reminded Bay of the clubs back in London, with the modelesque girls in charge of who can and cannot enter the party. Olivia gave their names and Bay thought World War Three was about to kick off when the woman asked to see Olivia's ID because she had been put down on the guest list as 'Oliver'.

'Shoes off, please!' commanded the woman, as she checked each girl's name off her piece of paper attached to a clipboard.

'Why?' barked Olivia. 'You think I'm going to leave my Louboutins under your supervision, really?'

'It's a pool party, no shoes around the pool,' she answered with a smile, as she cocked her head patronisingly like the Barbie doll in the *Toy Story* movies.

'Damn,' whispered Bay as they took a seat to remove their shoes. 'Do you think someone has created this rule because of the CCTV?'

'Probably,' Olivia replied, tucking her red-bottomed heels under her arm. 'No normal person would ask us to "remove your shoes" at a party. I mean it's absolutely feral. If we don't all get a verruca it'll be a miracle.' Olivia gave the floor a filthy look.

Molly, Mia and Bay went to hand their shoes to the girl with the checklist.

'Eww, no, don't give them to me,' she said, leaning away from the girls' shoes that were thrust towards her, fending them off with her clipboard like they were some kind of wild beasts. 'Leave them in the room on the left.' She pointed with the clipboard down the corridor.

The girls followed her orders and turned into the room on the left, which was covered in shoes, all over the floor, on the windowsill and on the furniture. There must have been over fifty pairs.

'Brilliant,' said Mia, sarcastically, as she carefully placed her own shoes in a little space on top of a chest of drawers.

'Olivia, get in here!' Molly summoned her friend into the room.

'No, I'm going to carry mine thank you very much. I'm not risking £750 of Italian leather stilettos leaving this party on some heifer's toes, thinking they were hers, or worse knowing they weren't hers and trying to nab mine!' Olivia hissed, gripping her own shoes even tighter.

'No, I mean we need you to look for the fake Gucci's.' At this point Molly was physically dragging Olivia into the shoe room.

'Ooh, there they are!' Mia called, pointing to a pair of white trainers with stripes on the sides over on the window ledge.

'No, sweetie, they are actual Gucci's. Exhibit A everyone, real Gucci's right there. We're looking for a pair as real as Mia's lips.' Olivia threw her head back in laughter at her own joke, resembling Basil Brush, before being poked in the ribs by Mia who didn't take kindly to her filler-filled lips being the butt of Olivia's joke.

'Wow, a lot of people have these Gucci's, don't they?' Bay observed, as the girls counted at least five other pairs of green and red striped white trainers.

'Of course they do, they are the number one trending item for both men and women on Vogue's spring style must-haves,' Olivia explained, as if it were common knowledge that everyone should know. Olivia tut-tutted loudly, sounding frustrated that she even needed to explain the popularity of the Gucci favourites.

'Ah, there!' she suddenly yelled, making the girls jump. Olivia was pointing to a bench at the back of the room that looked like it belonged in someone's garden and not inside a five-star mansion.

Mia waded through the copious pairs of shoes on the floor, stumbling over stilettos, slipping on sliders and tripping over trainers. She made it to the fake Gucci's and held them up for Olivia to inspect in further detail.

'Yup,' confirmed Olivia. 'These are the same fakes from the video and whoever owns them is in serious need of a leather insole and some Febreze shoe spray – Poo-ey.' She tossed the trainers back to Mia, who caught them by the laces and put them back where she had found them.

Bay had actually been quite looking forward to an afternoon in the sun. She knew they had come to find answers, but it all seemed to be coming to a head rather quickly. She suddenly went cold, and her body tensed as she realised that whoever the trainers belonged to was there at the pool party.

CHAPTER 25

'Life is like a swimming pool. You dive on in, but you don't know how deep it is.'

The house itself was stunning, not just from the outside but internally, as well. Although it was approaching thirty degrees outside, the house was built to withstand the heat and remained refreshingly cool inside thanks to the marbled floors and exposed white concrete walls. It had a kind of warehouse vibe rather than an Arabian feel, particularly when they reached the kitchen. The entire back wall was exposed brick. The white goods were all silver, industrial-looking machines, including the seven-ring gas hob and extractor fan that took central stage on a middle island. Matching silver utensils hung from the hood, like shiny pieces of jewellery at the Souk markets.

The whole back of the villa was open plan and the industrial kitchen continued into the rectangular lounge and dining area. The dining table was set up for over twenty people and was dressed like Prince William and Kate would be joining for dinner. It was all rather ostentatious with three knives on the right, three forks on the left, a side plate and spreader, a fork and spoon at the top and three glasses, yes - *three* glasses for each person arranged in a triangle on the right. The table itself was huge, about two metres wide and goodness knows how many long, covered in a hessian-style table-cloth that looked more like it was meant to hold pota-toes than several courses of a meal.

There was a selection of green plants in terracotta pots placed willy-nilly down the centre, interspersed with cream Jo Malone candles sat in silver dishes. The candles all looked brand new, as there was not a bit of wax out of place.

Behind the table, against the wall, were more terra-cotta plant pots filled with a variety of tropical-looking flora, some of which had huge sharp looking spikes towering into the air like tall African grasses. Others contained geranium-style pink flowers and one plant had leaves that spilled over the edges of its pot like octopus tentacles, making their way towards the floor. Bay made a mental note not to sit next to that one as it looked like it would try and poke you and she didn't need an exotic plant scaring the shit out of her when there was a murderer on the loose. Despite the creepy plant, Bay thought the set up was absolutely magnifi-cent and she took one more look before they all headed outside.

'How tacky,' commented Olivia, quite contrary to Bay's opinion. Olivia had been to more A-list parties than Bay, so perhaps she knew best.

If Olivia thought that was tacky, she was in for a treat as they walked out of the huge sliding concertina doors that were wide open to give that continuous indoor, outdoor feel. They were met with the most glorious outdoor space. This was where the party was at and people were milling about, covering every social spot in the garden. They were everywhere, from the wooden table and chairs with fat cream cushions and matching parasol on a raised hexagonal concrete plinth resembling a bandstand on the left, to an L-shaped white wicker outdoor sofa with navy padded seats and matching coffee table with glass top on the right. Last but not least, in the centre, was a huge oval-shaped swimming pool surrounded by very comfortable-looking sun loungers. The scene looked just like a Slim Aarons picture which Bay's friend, Jess, had on her wall in her hallway back in Cornwall. Bay had always gazed at it wondering what it felt like to be (a) present at such an exclusive event and (b) at such a boujie setting. She never expected to be like one of the women in the picture, engaging in *Poolside Gossip* as the artwork was entitled and yet, here she was stepping into that world.

The pool looked so welcoming, shimmering with a brilliant blue and was big enough to comfortably hold several large inflatable floats. Not the type that your nan would buy you from a tourist shop in Benidorm, but the kind only found on the grids of Instagram models and top DJs partying at the likes of Nikki Beach. The pool sported the stereotypical pink flamingo, a gold swan and a large white unicorn and they were being ridden by a trio of extension-wearing blondes who all had equally as unnecessary large inflatables of their own bulging from their chests, held up by stringy bikini tops that were too small. Any sudden movements and the scene would transition from pool paradise to Playboy!

It was all too much for Olivia, who found the whole thing over the top and tasteless. She didn't even need to say it, the picture on her face spoke a thousand words as she wrinkled her nose and shook her head in disapproval.

'Oh my days! Is that Lindsay Lohan?' asked Mia, grabbing Bay's arm, signalling with her elbow towards a redhead jigging away next to the DJ's booth. She was trying to be subtle but Bay thought it was quite the opposite and turned her back on the Lindsay lookalike in case it actually *was* her and she asked for them to be removed for harassing her.

'Ooh, it does look like her, this is deffo worthy of a check in,' Molly said excitedly as she started tapping on her phone. 'I wonder what other celebs have been here, I bet lots, let's see.' Molly began scrolling through the location check-ins on Instagram. They could see some people from today including the DJ, a guy in a red Hawaiian shirt and the Insta-hoes on the inflatables who were currently holding the top spots for 'likes'. She scrolled further down to find Daniel Radcliffe AKA Harry Potter and also Ed Sheeran who had previously posted at that very location.

'Hold on, go back up,' Mia demanded, suddenly. Molly swiped the other way, slowly. 'There, that one.'

Mia clicked on the picture of a mousy-brown haired, modelesque girl who had taken a completely make-up-free selfie, still looking like a rock star in front of the pool.

'Who's that? I don't recognise her, is she a model?' asked Bay, peering at the picture. The date it was posted was June last year.

'No, it's that girl that drowned at that party,' Mia said, spreading her thumb and forefinger out over the image to enlarge it.

'Oh yeah, it's definitely her,' confirmed Molly, who had now placed her sunglasses on her head and was squinting at her phone to get a better look.

'No way, let's see!' Olivia grabbed the phone. She had previously poopooed the story as being boring when they'd discussed it at their table at the Parsons Green pub.

'But the drowning was ruled as caused by an excessive amount of drugs in her bloodstream though,' Molly reminded them of the story.

'Yes, but don't you remember, her friends had given interviews saying that she never touched anything like that?' Mia was trying to pull up articles on her phone.

'Oh please, that's because when anyone's death is drug-related, all the nearest and dearest pop up in *the Sun* professing their innocence and purity because they don't want to admit they were actually a coke head,' Olivia rattled off harshly. 'How else do you suppose the drugs got there?' she questioned Mia and Molly, who were clearly not amused by her previous statement.

'Exactly, maybe it was put there by someone else, say like a sleeping pill in a bottle of water!' Mia reminded them of their close encounter earlier that day.

'But how does she relate to any of this?' asked Bay, assessing the partygoers in the pool area for any sort of suspicious activity. There was a boy with a very suspicious-looking cigarette but other than that everyone was either flaunting their bodies, flexing their muscles or sipping a strong drink.

'Girls!' It was Carl Baker, running towards them in his white shorts and navy tee shirt. 'Glad you could make it. Are you staying for supper?' he asked, doing weird dad-style moves to the beat of the DJ's dance music that was blaring across the garden.

Bay thought he looked considerably less hot than she thought the night before. She clearly must have been wearing her wine goggles.

'Of course,' replied Mìa with a smile. 'Can't wait, what a beautiful setting.'

'Great. We'll take our seats at the dining table in about an hour, once I get the rest of this lot to fuck off.' He laughed and then began coughing like he'd inhaled too quickly.

'Do you often have parties here?' Bay took the opportunity to try and find out more about the party last year.

'Yeah, whenever I'm in Dubai I rent this place, it's like my second home. I've been coming here every year to see my son who lives in Australia, it's basically a halfway point for us. And it makes a great party venue, don't you think?' He clapped his hands together.

'Yeah, until someone drowns,' Olivia blurted out, in her true straight-to-the-point style.

'Oh that. Well, didn't anyone teach you that if you dabble with drugs you're going to come to a sticky end?' Carl directed his words towards Olivia, who never liked being talked down to or told what to do.

'Or dabble with the wrong people?' she calmly responded, her lips curving up at the edges in a menacing smile.

'Indeed,' Carl's delivery was stern and slightly less friendly than his usual banter. With that he carried on dancing past the girls, shaking his hands like he had a set of invisible maracas.

'Liv, knock it off. Please don't take your hangover out on the guy who is going to control my life for the next year,' snapped Mia, looking red in the face either from anger or embarrassment or both.

'Umm, hello?' Olivia looked from Mia, to Molly, to Bay. 'Are you all blind? I think Mr Carl Baker has a lot to answer for. I'm glad we're staying for dinner as I've got plenty more questions for him where that came from.' She rubbed her hands together like a villain with a plan.

'What on earth are you talking about? Are we missing the point?' Molly looked around at Mia and Bay to support her blank expression and to validate that she wasn't completely stupid.

'I think he knows a hell of a lot more. It was his party where that poor girl drowned and his party where Amy fell off the roof. Either he knows more than we think, or he seriously needs to review his health and safety contracts.' Olivia did make a fair point.

'Maybe he can explain this, too.' Mia had finally got a patch of signal to her phone and the article about the girl who drowned had managed to open. 'It says her name was Annabelle Van Lissen, an up-and-coming model who was found out to be less of a model and more of an escort. She was secretly seducing a string of wealthy men around the world and guess who she had been dating before she died?' Mia paused for effect and everyone held their breath, not imagining for the life of them who it could be.

'Only Daniel Baker, son of Director Carl Baker.'

CHAPTER 26

*'It isn't so much what is on
the dinner table that matters,
it's who is in the chairs.'*

The hour flew by and as the last of the pool party stragglers were escorted out by the woman with the clipboard (much to their disappointment), the remaining select few took their seats at the dinner table. Outside, the staff were removing various inflatable unicorns, swans and ducks from the pool and stacking them up out of the way and generally trying to restore some sort of order to the landscaped garden area.

The VIP guests, as Olivia had described the chosen few who had been selected to stay for supper, consisted of the same batch from the night before plus a few more 'it' girls and actor types.

The girls hadn't spoken to Max or his dad since the night before, as they were both still high up on the suspect list. Max was quite fidgety and unsettled on his side of the table, probably because he'd drawn the short straw and was the one sat the closest to the prickly plant.

Before heading to dinner the guests had been told that they could now put their shoes back on but in the melee of people leaving and darting in and out of the shoe room, they had lost track of the fake Gucci's, although the general consensus of the girls was that they were now firmly on the feet of one of the people sat round the table with them. The only issue was that the table was covered from top to toe with the hessian cloth, blocking any view of the feet underneath.

'You know the only way we're going to be able to sort this whole thing out is to somehow get under the table,' Olivia whispered, barely moving her mouth, like a ventriloquist.

This time the girls had chosen to huddle round one end of the table so they could discuss matters more discreetly without any other guests taking too much notice of them.

'And how do you suppose we do that? Crawl around on our hands and knees under the tablecloth like children?' Mia suggested sarcastically.

'Precisely,' smirked Olivia, as she knocked one of her three forks to the floor. It clattered loudly on to the marbled tiles, causing everyone at the table to stop their conversations and look round in the direction of Olivia.

'Really discreet,' Mia mouthed at Olivia.

'Oopsie!' Olivia slid down her chair rather seductively and disappeared out of sight under the table.

Bay could hear Olivia rummaging around trying to break through the tablecloth, she could only imagine the mass of legs and feet Olivia would be met with.

'Oh!' jumped one of Carl's business friends, almost leaving his seat. Olivia must have accidentally touched him whilst roaming around on the floor.

Mia put her head onto the table in front of her to shield herself from Olivia's further embarrassment.

'What is going on down here?' Carl now had his face under the tablecloth, too. It must have made Olivia jump as her head hit the table so hard that the glasses all chimed as they knocked together.

'For fuck's sake.' Bay needed to sort this out and she too popped her head under the tablecloth. It was surprisingly dark under there, but she could just about make out Olivia on her hands and knees at the other end, as well as Carl's head which was laughing now. Thank goodness he was finding this entertaining and not absolutely absurd, she thought, feeling slightly relieved.

'Liv!' Bay clicked her fingers like she was calling back a naughty puppy. Olivia began crawling back towards Bay's end of the table at speed. Her skirt being so short, she was probably flashing Carl, who was still grinning at the other end.

'What the actual fuck were you thinking? Have you gone completely mad?' Mia snapped as Olivia appeared from under the tablecloth and clambered back up to her seat.

Olivia lifted up the fork in success to show the retrieved item to the confused looking faces. Once everyone slowly started resuming their various conversations and Mia's red face had returned to a normal colour, Bay decided it was safe to speak again.

'So, did you see the shoes?' Bay asked in a hushed tone.

'God no, it was far too dark! I couldn't see a thing. Pretty sure I grabbed someone's actual leg thinking it was a table leg!' Olivia, for once, also looked slightly embarrassed by her actions. 'Thank God that's all I grabbed, you know what I mean?' She winked.

'Brilliant, so that little show was all for nothing.' Mia shook her head in frustration and leant back in her chair, throwing her hands behind her head. As she did so she knocked a glass out of Molly's hands, and it fell to the floor and shattered.

Olivia couldn't help but let out a snort at the irony of the last few minutes, what a comedy of errors. They couldn't have drawn more attention to themselves if they'd tried!

All three of the men on the opposite side of the table, Max, Michael and Carl got up to collect the pieces of glass and take them out to the bin in the kitchen.

'There they are!' hissed Molly pointing at the three men. 'The shoes!'

'On who?' Mia turned her body round quickly to look in the direction of the men who had left the kitchen and were carrying the overflowing bin out into the hallway.

'I don't know. I just saw them on someone's feet as they headed for the kitchen. I wasn't really paying attention, but they were wearing shorts.' Molly looked thrilled with her discovery like a child who had just won a giant stuffed toy at the fair.

'All three of them are wearing shorts, as we're at a pool party, so that's great, babe. Well done, eyes like a hawk this one,' Olivia said, sarcastically pointing her thumb towards Molly.

'At least she's not blind and actually spotted the shoes without having to make a fool of herself by crawling around under the table at dinner!' Mia retorted.

In the action, Bay had taken it upon herself, helped by her journalistic curiosity, to follow the three men out into the hallway when she saw them leave the kitchen. She was sick of the anxious feeling that had been engulfing her ever since Amy's death. It had started off, albeit a serious matter, as a bit of an adventure with her new friends but since realising they were somehow caught up in a dangerous situation since the accident at Mia's speech at the flower show and nearly being drugged in their own hotel room, she was becoming exhausted of having to live life watching her back and being suspicious of every Tom, Dick and Harry that crossed her path. She had already put a plan into action at the dinner table which she hoped was about to unfold to help catch the murderer, now all she had to do was figure out who the murderer was.

When she reached the hallway, the three men were nowhere to be seen. She looked around to see where they could have gone, but there was no sign of anyone, not even the clipboard girl. Bay decided to go upstairs to use the restroom at the top of the stairs anyway. There were no lights on and despite it still being pretty light outside, all the blinds were shut.

Suddenly, the door to the bathroom swung open creating a shaft of light and someone came out. Bay couldn't make out who it was but heard a man's voice say, 'That's it, you two just stay there, whilst I figure out what to do next.' It was not said in a friendly voice like *you two stay there whilst I go and sort out the pudding* way but more a *stay there whilst I take care of my evil plan* way. It couldn't have sounded more sinister if the perpetrator had finished the sentence with a 'muhahahaha!'

Knowing that something was not quite right, Bay darted into a room on the left, stubbing her toe on a chest of drawers just inside the door with a thud. The pain was excruciating but she had to stifle a grunt as she heard heavy footsteps heading in her direction. She scrambled around, frantically trying to find somewhere to hide. Eventually, she slid under the bed which she instantly regretted. After watching so many horror films, she remembered that it did not end well for the majority of characters who hid under beds. She held her breath as someone entered the room. It was still too dark to see who it was but as frightening as it was, Bay thought at least if it was too dark for her to see them, they in turn would not be able to see her.

The person walked straight past the bed towards the window and pulled at the roller blind. Light crept into the room, the sun starting to fill every nook and cranny like water rushing into a canal lock. Just as Bay was about to look in the direction of the window to see if she could now make out who it was, there was a knock on the door and Mia's voice said, 'Hey Bay, are you in there?'

Bay couldn't possibly reveal her hiding space now; it would be far too bizarre for her to suddenly pop out from under the bed like one of those strippers out of a stag party cake. Although she couldn't establish if the person at the other side of the room was a danger or not, she thought she'd be safest to observe from under the bed, keeping a watchful eye on Mia and be ready to jump in if necessary. Mia's feet entered the room.

'Oh hi,' Mia said in a friendly manner to the other person, who to Bay's disappointment did not respond. Mia's feet in their gold-heeled sandals crossed the room and Bay followed them over to the window which led out on to a balcony.

This was it, Bay thought, time for her to lay eyes on whoever it was. She recalled from the film *Taken* that you needed to remember every single bit of detail about someone as everything you saw could be a useful and important clue and possibly save your life. As she mentally noted what she could see, Bay thought she was being slightly dramatic as if a pair of hairy legs and Gucci trainers would be a matter of life or death.

Fake Gucci trainers. Bay was horrified as she saw them at the end of the hairy legs and realised she had found the murderer.

CHAPTER 27

'Don't let anyone with bad shoes
tell you how to live your life.'

'A my!' a man's voice cried. 'Oh my God, sorry, I mean Mia. Gosh you two really do look alike, or *did* look alike I suppose I should have said,' he continued, not as apologetically as one would have hoped if you'd just confused someone with a dead person.

By now the 'fake Gucci man' and Mia were stood out on the balcony. Bay wondered if this was her time to come out from under the bed and escape back to the safety of the dinner party downstairs. She let the words that he'd said sink into her head as she desperately tried to place the muffled voice. She knew she should recognise it, but was it Michael, Carl or Max? Whoever it was, she couldn't believe how stupid they were to put their big, fake-Gucci-wearing feet in it and confuse Mia with Amy.

Then it suddenly hit her – There was no way Mia's own boyfriend, Max, would ever confuse her with Amy, nor would Max's dad which only left one person. Carl Baker. Then another wave of realisation swept over her. What if Amy had actually been mistaken for Mia on the rooftop and whoever committed such an awful crime was meant to get rid of Mia. They did after all look identical, particularly on that night; people had been mixing them up all over the place.

Bay's mind was working overtime. Why Mia and why Carl? She started piecing bits together. Carl had given the role in the film to Mia on the day Bay had gone to the audition with her so, for some reason, Carl no longer wanted her in his film... but why? Maybe he saw Mia and Bachelor Ben becoming close, but how? Then she remembered when she had been sat in the car waiting to leave the audition and Mia had disappeared with Bachelor Ben out of sight, they were closely followed by Carl who had stopped very abruptly when he looked around the corner where Ben and Mia had gone.

That's it, Bay concluded. He must have seen Mia and Ben getting close. Of course, if that got out before filming even began it would ruin the reputation and standing of the film company and, in turn, Carl Baker would lose his notable recognition as a serious classic five-star film maker. Having an ex-reality star was risky to start with but to have a possible affair conducted on set between the main actors would be ruinous and make him a laughing stock in the industry. Carl would kiss goodbye to any major profit.

It all began to make sense. Carl had solved one problem of the model in the pool embarrassing his son a year earlier, and once he'd got away with *that* murder, he'd thought that disposing of his obstacles was easier than he'd imagined. Being such a well-known and respected figure of society meant that he would be the last suspect on anyone's mind. And the attempted murder of Mia at the flower show also tied in with his involvement, as who knew Mia was there? Carl, of course. And who asked the girls to attend a paid for trip to Dubai just after the attempted murder? Carl again.

But what about the fake Gucci trainers? Surely Carl had enough money to afford the real thing? Then again when Bay had first met him, he had been wearing a mafia-style pinstripe suit that wasn't remotely fashionable. He clearly needed to fire his personal stylist, if he even had one.

Before Bay could think of any more evidence to string together, her focus was turned back to the balcony where Carl now had hold of Mia by her arms.

'Just like déjà vu this, isn't it?' His now slimy-sounding voice made Bay shudder and he started to shake Mia from side to side, trying to overpower her. However, he had under-estimated her strength which, for a fiery Italian who had committed many hours to the gym, was hardly surprising. She was never going to be an easy target.

'Mia!' called Bay loudly clawing at the floor to get out from under the bed as quickly as possible.

Both Carl and Mia turned round in shock, not expecting someone else to be in the room and crawling out of nowhere.

Carl, seeing the opportunity, took advantage of the distraction and flipped Mia right over the edge of the balcony before anyone had time to do anything.

Bay screamed as she was knocked down herself by three burly policemen who stormed in, followed closely by Olivia. It could not have been better timing at they literally caught Carl red-handed.

Bay and Olivia rushed over to the balcony and peered over in dread, only to see the remaining dinner guests gathered outside. There was no sign of Mia. Bay scanned the scene, desperately trying to catch a glimpse of the body of their friend, when her attention was caught by a gentleman pulling someone out of the pool. She looked again at the group of onlookers, but no-one looked panicked or in need of counselling having witnessed a person plunging to their death. The group, in fact, began laughing and applauding and the girls realised it was Mia climbing out of the pool. Bay tried to make sense of the scene and realised that when the staff removed the inflatables from the pool and stacked them on top of each other under the balcony they had acted as a bouncy castle, catching Mia and catapulting her straight into the pool.

Olivia gave a dramatic outpouring of air in a huge sigh, as if she had been holding her breath for a long time.

'Was it you that called the police?' asked Bay, looking at Olivia and then at the police, who placed handcuffs on Carl and marched him downstairs.

'Yup,' Olivia nodded proudly, basking in her newfound heroic glory. 'I knew something was up, you missed Molly passing out!'

Bay then remembered her own earlier plan that she had started to put into action when she had found the sleeping pills still in her bag from the morning. She'd put one of the pills into one of the girls' drinks to use as evidence. Her plan was to frame the murderer once they had identified their suspect, by drugging one of the girls and then calling the police with a tip-off of drugs at a party. The police took this very seriously in Dubai and they would have certainly arrived at the party in haste. Bay knew they would not take the suspicions of four girls of a murderer as seriously without any evidence but would be there on the double if illegal substances were involved. Bay then intended to plant the remainder of the sleeping pills on their suspected murderer and she suddenly remembered that she had not yet put this second part of her plan into action so she hurried off downstairs to where the police were escorting Carl off the premises.

She ran up to them, flailing her arms, thanking them profusely for coming so quickly and generally singing their praises to such an extent that they lapped up the attention and did not notice her slipping the sleeping tablets into Carl's back pocket, just to ensure there was no way he could wriggle out of any charges.

Sure, it was tampering with evidence and possibly could be seen as trying to frame someone, but when the person you were setting up was a nasty, murdering piece of work, Bay saw it as simply doing her public duty and nudging the world in the right direction.

CHAPTER 28

'The Last Table in the Sun'

B ay was the first to arrive and headed for their usual table to hold fort. It was as if no-one else ever wanted the last table in the sun. It was always there, basking in the full heat of the still-hot evening London sunlight.

They had flown back from Dubai the day after the pool party events and Carl's arrest. Although they weren't due to leave until two days later, they'd wanted to escape back to London. They'd put their flights on Olivia's credit card and they would probably all be indebted to her for the rest of their lives.

Bay thought she would start the payback by purchasing the first of what was likely to be many bottles of wine for the evening ahead. She ordered with a passing waiter, not wanting to abandon their favourite table.

Olivia was the next to arrive, waving with her entire arm and yelling a 'Cooee!' greeting as she trotted across the road. It was no wonder people called her an attention seeker, although Olivia would deny it until the end of time.

She was dressed head to toe in white, with flared white trousers, nude wedges, a white knitted cami top and to finish off her look, a white fedora hat. She flopped down on one of the wooden chairs and unscrewed the bottle of rosé that had just arrived. She poured it into the four wine glasses and popped the small remainder in the bottle back into the ice bucket which gleamed in the sun.

'Ah.' Olivia sipped the refreshing liquid. 'Chin, chin.' She clinked Bay's glass with her own. 'What a crazy few days,' she sighed, leaning back in her chair.

Molly and Mia arrived together, arm in arm and giggling as they merrily bounced along the pavement. They were both in summer dresses, Molly in a baby pink floral number and Mia in a white wrap dress with black polka dots.

'Hey!' They waved, with grins.

Bay thought how nice it was to see everyone smiling again like they had done before it all went so epically downhill. They joined Bay and Olivia and began tucking straight into their wine. No surprises there!

'How are you feeling now, Mol?' Bay asked, rubbing Molly's back. She stopped quickly, thinking it may have been a little patronising.

'She's fine, no thanks to you. Do we need to keep an eye on all our drinks nowadays, Bay, or are your drug baron days over?' Olivia took it on herself to answer on behalf of Molly, adding one of her usual glib quips.

Bay had decided to tell the girls about her involvement with knocking out Molly with half a sleeping pill and slipping the rest of the packet into Carl's pocket. She simply couldn't hide it from her new best friends even though sharing any form of secret with Olivia was dodgy. She'd learnt that in primary school when she'd said that she'd fancied Sam Holland, a boy in the year above and although Olivia had promised not to say anything, within minutes of their conversation, about four other children had come up to Bay, singing 'Sam and Bay sitting in a tree ...'

Speaking of fancying people, due to the stress of the last few days, not to mention the fact that they could have been history if Carl had had his way, Bay had one of those life-affirming moments. You know, the ones where you dissect every aspect of your life and try to find out what you really want. It turned out that Bay enjoyed the fast-paced London life but didn't want to work in the competitive rat race that was the media. So, when she returned from Dubai, as soon as she was allowed to turn on her phone in the airport, she'd messaged Ollie, the dog walker she had met in the park. She was due to meet him tomorrow to discuss working together in the dog-walking business. Tomorrow she was also viewing an apartment on Fulham Road. It was an en suite room in a three-bed flat, sharing with a guy who was a chef and a girl who taught yoga.

Although she had enjoyed living with Olivia, her life was very full-on, and Bay was looking forward to having her own space. She felt ready for the next chapter of her London adventure. Hopefully, it would involve less drama and escapes from death.

The bond she had made with Mia, Molly and her old pal Olivia was one that would remain forever. You don't easily forget the times you were quivering in fear of your life. It had taken teamwork, dedication, determination and fierce heroism from the four girls and it would not have been possible without any of them.

As if they had all been thinking the same thing, the four girls began grinning at one another with Cheshire cat smiles that quickly turned to laughter, for no particular reason. This was a little goodbye drink for now as Mia was heading to Italy for the rest of the summer with Max so they could spend some time together. She had confessed to her flirting advances with Ben, which of course hadn't gone down well at first, but Mia had said they both had things to work on. Molly was due to move in with Archie, who coincidently was no longer Mia's agent as Mia had decided to stick to Instagram modelling rather than acting and Olivia, in true Olivia style, had a diary full of mingling, A-list parties and brand launches. 'She couldn't possibly fit in anything else', in her words, which basically meant that she would be pissed by about 3pm every day for the foreseeable future!

'Cheers,' hollered Bay, raising her glass.

'To what?' Olivia was only half paying attention as she was tapping away on her phone.

'To us!' replied the other three girls. Mia even managed to force the phone out of Olivia's hands and put it face down on the table.

'Well duh!' Olivia joined in and raised her glass too.

They finished the last of the bottle just as the sun disappeared behind a tree. The last table in the sun was now no longer lit up and sat in the cooler shade like the rest of the pub. Bay got up to leave, but paused to admire the pink sunset that was forming so beautifully.

'Red sky at night, shepherd's delight,' she quoted the well-known rhyme and felt relaxed that the world was confirming tomorrow would be a good day.

'Another bottle?' asked Olivia, with puppy dog eyes.

'Oh, go on then!' Bay sat back down in her chair and watched the sun set from her new favourite spot in the world.

End

ACKNOWLEDGEMENTS

I've always loved to read and write for as long as I can remember first holding a pencil! I was always scribbling away ideas or storylines after school and I remember once writing a short story in primary school that I never finished because I got too excited and couldn't contain my ideas and it went on and on and on.

It has always been on my bucket list and in 'my things to do in the New Year' goals since circa the millennium. Well, it's 2019 and I can finally put a big tick to that one!

So thank you first and always to my Mum and Dad for not thinking I was insane to write an entire book and for encouraging me to, not only pursue this dream, but every other dream I ever had; being an international DJ, becoming a singer, creating prosthetics for theatre productions, which are all still pending!

Secondly, to my English teachers who I must have annoyed the hell out of by telling them my many story ideas or giving them snippets of 'works in progress' to read when I'm sure they had better things to be doing.

In particular Mr Byford and Mrs Jordan at Tower House, who could see my passion for literature and helped me to reach my potential.

To my boyfriend Luke, I'm sorry for taking up your time on our holiday to Greece by continuously reading you chapter after chapter of my work, whether you wanted to hear it or not! And for ignoring you for most of the 'holiday' whilst I sat by the pool and wrote this book.

Thanks also to Tim at the Livermead House Hotel for, unbeknownst to him, giving me the title of this book in passing conversation. Once I had the title, there was no stopping me.

Continuing with the hotel theme, also a big shout out to everyone at the Atrium Prestige Hotel in Rhodes, Greece where I wrote most of this book and who kept me supplied with pens! You really looked after us and we enjoyed every minute of our stay. Hopefully we will be back soon!

To every author who has written a book that I have got completely lost in which inspired me to even want to take on this challenge in the first place.

To everyone who also has 'writing a book' on their bucket list, this one's for you and I hope it brings you the strength, courage and 'oh fuck it, just do it' attitude to write your own story.

And last but not least, thanks to each and every one of you who has bought and read this book. You've fulfilled a dream!

About the Author

Lexie grew up by the coast in Torquay, Devon and filled her childhood with writing (mainly about dogs), whether in school or at home, when she probably should have been doing homework!

Lexie moved to London when she was 18 to pursue various ambitions such as being a singer, a presenter, a DJ and a hair, make-up and prosthetics artist (all still pending by the way!). And writing a book has been on Lexie's bucket list and one of her 'things to do in the New Year' goals since circa the millennium. Well it's 2019 and she can finally put a big tick to that one!

'The Last Table in the Sun' is Lexie's debut novel. Inspired by a love of reading book after book whilst on holiday in the sun written by other female authors such as Sophie Kinsella, focussing on female protagonists and their adventures. Also, being a fan of darker dramatic comedies like 'Desperate Housewives' and 'Pretty Little Liars', the mix of girly 'Sex and The City'-esque glamour with a hint of murder mystery is where 'The Last Table in the Sun' sits.

Lexie lives in West London with her boyfriend Luke and their 3 year old toy poodle, Bali, named after the Indonesian Island they visited and fell in love with. She works as a radio presenter every Thursday from 10am-1pm on local station Riverside Radio, hosting a fun magazine style show full of celebrity gossip, fashion, classic throwback tunes as well as current chart toppers. When not on the radio Lexie dabbles in property, completing her first development project in 2018 and another one set to complete in the coming months. She also assists others, as a property finder, to locate their new home in London.

You'll find Lexie and Bali in one of the many dog friendly, West London eateries having a glass of Prosecco or an afternoon tea, or simply taking a stroll along the river.

Social Media:
Website / Blog: www.lexiecarducci.co.uk
Instagram: www.instagram.com/lexiecarducci
Twitter: www.twitter.com/lexiecarducci